Entr@pment

Entr@pment

A High School Comedy in Chat

M. Spooner

Margaret K. McElderry Books

New York London Toronto Sydney

Margaret K. McElderry Books
An imprint of Simon & Schuster Children's Publishing Division
1230 Avenue of the Americas, New York, New York 10020
Book design by Mike Rosamilia
The text for this book is set in Gotham.
Manufactured in the United States of America
10 9 8 7 6 5 4 3 2 1
Library of Congress Cataloging-in-Publication Data
Spooner, Michael.
Entr@pment : a high school comedy in chat /
M. Spooner.
p. cm.
Summary: Two teenage girls assume false identities online in
order to test the fidelity of their boyfriends. Told in the form
of chat room communications.
ISBN: 978-1-4169-5889-5 (hardcover)
[1. Online identities—Fiction. 2. Impostors and imposture—
Fiction. 3. Dating (Social customs)—Fiction. 4. Online chat
groups—Fiction. 5. Interpersonal relations—Fiction.
6. Friendship—Fiction.] I. Title. II. Title: Entrapment.
PZ7.S7638En 2009
[Fic]—dc22
2008022944

FIRST
EDITION

✉ IM from the Author

meshikee: dedicated to the memory of Molly Spooner, who loved both opera and young people—*come scoglio* (like a rock).

meshikee: with many thanks to Syl and Isaac for the very idea, to Joyce and David for the lake effect, to Kylee and Jennifer for the feedback, and to Stephen and Lisa for believing in it.

meshikee: um, with apologies to Mozart and da Ponte.

Entr@pment

Young Love
25 MAY

We will vow to one another
there will never be another
—Cartey and Joyner, lame old love song

Peace and joy, camper. Spring has sprung, and young hearts have turned to thoughts of love—just as Your Uncle Jerry predicted. Young love. It's pathetic. Sad and sorry. Call it what you will, as long as it rhymes with "lame."

Now, don't jump to your keyboard, don't flame Your Uncle Jerry. Hear me out. Because I am just as fond of love's longing gaze as anyone. Uncle Jerry adores mouth-breathing and half-wit conversation. I *live* to hear young campers pour out the poetry of passion from their shallow, shallow souls.

Because Uncle Jerry knows what follows. And there is nothing—nothing—more entertaining than the flash of fury in a young girl's eye when she finds her boy in the arms of her own best friend.

Cruel, you say? Heartless? Not at all. I enjoy this only because I know it is the prelude to wisdom. Ah, yes, young lovers, I've had a love of my own. Worst eight hours of my life.

Pay attention—that's a joke. I say, that's a joke, son.

Oh. Sorry, camper girl, did you really think he could be true? Sorry, camper guy, did she say she'd save herself for you? Care to gamble on it? Turn your back and trust her if you dare. That's the only way to know.

Here's Your Uncle Jerry's wager (you know how Uncle Jerry loves a wager): I bet your lover will not love you still, young miss; your sweetheart will not sigh for you, young sir.

Young love will have another love next year.

Peace and joy.

CHAPTER 1
conspiracy

GURLGANG ROOM

MAY 26 07:15 PM

Ms.T has entered

Ms.T: yo bliss, you there?

bliss4u: hey T

Ms.T: hey girl

bliss4u: so what u guys do after the game?

gothling has entered

bliss4u: hey annie

gothling: **yo**

Ms.T: we did nothing special. went to the mall

bliss4u: again with the mall? <sigh sigh sigh>

Ms.T:	ok, so he takes it slow. he likes the simple pleasures. i can totally live with it
gothling:	**who does? beau?**
bliss4u:	of course...
Ms.T:	plus he's a little afraid of me. i like that in a boy toy. >:)
bliss4u:	lol
Ms.T:	you think it's the dreds?
bliss4u:	or the grades =)
gothling:	**or yr death-2-the-oppressor politics**
bliss4u:	totally. i luuvvvv T, but i don't get half the stuff she says...
gothling:	**T is like alicia keys meets whoopi goldberg**
Ms.T:	oh great, i'm a sickly sweet soul singer and a saggy, middle-aged comic
gothling:	**but a leftist saggy, middle-aged sickly sweet comic soul star**
bliss4u:	what's leftist, anyway?
gothling:	**still, there's the beau boy. i thought brainy girls went for the star quarterback**
Ms.T:	we know what you think, dear
gothling:	**beau is what? like backup to the backup tight end? what's up with that?**
bliss4u:	lol. but he's a hottie in football pants. :->
gothling:	**but see: is he good enough for our Tamra? i'm just sayin...**
Ms.T:	he's a sweetie! and he's real. i don't need brilliant, and I sure don't need hollywood
gothling:	**u just like him because u can control him**

Ms.T:	ouch
bliss4u:	not nice, annie
Ms.T:	like with your record, you should choose a guy for me? i'm just sayin...
bliss4u:	oh snap! i am so not getting between u 2nite
gothling:	**whatever**
bliss4u:	let's b nice, k? {{annie}} {{tamra}} k??
gothling:	**k, can we just not talk about boys right now?**
bliss4u:	sure. let's talk about me!
Ms.T:	right. let's be nice to poor annie. she's all alone, and she's done her hair black again
gothling:	**i'm not alone, prissy. i'm single. maybe u've heard of that**
bliss4u:	well, um... certain people think ur bitter and cold. i don't know where i heard that
gothling:	**people get the strangest ideas**
bliss4u:	anyway, u were too good for... he who must not be named
Ms.T:	well, and too intense, duh. what were you thinking, girl?
gothling:	**wouldn't wanna be intense. the boys r SO easily threatened**
bliss4u:	mitchie's not
gothling:	**we're not talking about boys, k?**
bliss4u:	sure, but who likes intense? who does that really work with, annie?
gothling:	**clearly, no one**
Ms.T:	anyway, annie hates all men this year. you said a year, right annie? :)

gothling:	**back off, u** **listen, i am not a man-hater. i am simply willing 2** **learn from experience. unlike some people**
Ms.T:	and you've learned what? um... tattoos, black nails, and a tongue stud attract men of intellect and refinement?
gothling:	**no, dred-girl. i have learned that none of that** **matters. u can't trust em, anyway. the wretches**
bliss4u:	ok, sugar. but we can't all stay as angry as u
gothling:	**ok baby. but i'm just wiser, not angry. see me** **smile : -**
bliss4u:	now see? that's really nice. she doesn't hate anyone
Ms.T:	she only finds them wretched
gothling:	**oh, gimme a break. i LIKE lots of guys. i just think** **they're dumb as a box of rocks**
bliss4u:	puhleeeze. mitch is really really smart
gothling:	**not about what matters. oh sigh, what do i know?** **i'm the one who fell for what's his name. voldemort**
Ms.T:	seems like i was just making that point
gothling:	**shut up, u. but that's it. never again. u just can't** **trust em**
Ms.T:	any of them?
gothling:	**any of em. any of em**
bliss4u:	but he was only 1, annie
gothling:	**sure, but they all... forget it. u guys are just** **pushing my buttons today**
bliss4u:	{annie} what?
gothling:	**i dunno. they're just morons. geeks and jocks** **and gangstas and all of them. i hate how easy** **they have it**

Ms.T:	how easy?
gothling:	**easy peasy. they don't even know—that's why they can't be trusted. the world revolves around them, and they can't even see it**
Ms.T:	that's what i'm talking about. institutional sexism
gothling:	**if they could even SEE it, i could cut them some slack**
bliss4u:	mitch isn't that way. he treats me really nice
gothling:	**ok, listen, sugar, 1) ur da perky blonde bomb of the universe**
bliss4u:	awww
Ms.T:	but how can you stand those airheads on cheer squad? brrr.
bliss4u:	come on. they're fun!
gothling:	**2) mitch is like chief geek of the chess club (though i admit he cleans up good)**
bliss4u:	ok, he didn't WANT to be president. that was Mrs Fafner
gothling:	**therefore 3) he would be insane not to worship u**
bliss4u:	well, true... =)
gothling:	**but 4) if yr worst enemy breathed in his ear, he'd follow her right 2 the backseat**
Ms.T:	maybe...
bliss4u:	u mean kami day? she wouldn't dare!!
Ms.T:	ROTFL. i just sprayed coke on my keyboard
gothling:	**um, bliss? u may be missing my point, dear**
bliss4u:	besides, 5) mitch doesn't even like her, so there!
Ms.T:	lol <cough cough cough>

bliss4u:	what? WHAT??
Ms.T:	no, i'm with u. mitch and kami? never happen
bliss4u:	that's what i'm sayin
gothling:	**T, ur not helping**
Ms.T:	or mitch and frankie? no worries there, either, am i right?
bliss4u:	totally. my 2nd worst enemy
Ms.T:	lol
bliss4u:	WHAT already???
gothling:	**okay, chickies, listen up. u people need 2 learn a lesson here**
Ms.T:	yes, mum, we listening
gothling:	**i'll make u a little wager, my pretties, 2 see who's right about the dumber sex <rubbing hands evilly>**
Ms.T:	annie loves a wager
bliss4u:	what wager?
gothling:	**let's just test yr 2 handsome units. see how much u can really trust them**
Ms.T:	ah... velly interesting. please to go on
gothling:	**but u have 2 put yrselves totally in my cynical scheming hands. understand? u must do exactly as i say, or u lose the bet**
bliss4u:	wait wait. what do u mean "how much we can trust them"?
gothling:	**trust means trust**
Ms.T:	i think annie's going to steal your boyfriend, honey
gothling:	**eww**

bliss4u:	that can't be legal... =)
Ms.T:	both of ours. she'll woo them away from us
gothling:	**sick bags on standby**
Ms.T:	no seriously, u think i can't trust beau tanner, star backup to the backup tight end?
gothling:	**that would be the general idea. u in or u out?**
bliss4u:	but i still need 2 hear the bet
gothling:	**well, it's obvious, isn't it? u guys disappear, and 2 mysterious young hotties slide in 2 take yr places**
Ms.T:	TRY to take our places
gothling:	**whatever**
bliss4u:	wait. who r they?
gothling:	**who?**
bliss4u:	them
gothling:	**them who?**
bliss4u:	them! who r THEY??
gothling:	**what? they're u, duh!!**
bliss4u:	what??
gothling:	**YOU**
Ms.T:	annie, let me do this.
	bliss. darlin. here's the deal
	you and i PRETEND to go away. mitch and beau are heartbroken, right?
bliss4u:	right...
Ms.T:	we make them promise to be good till we come back, ok?
bliss4u:	sure. k. then what?

Ms.T:	then we PRETEND to be someone else, and try to break them down
gothling:	**there u go**
bliss4u:	but how do we...? i mean, if they see us...
Ms.T:	true. um, Annie? online? we make up identities and hit on them from there?
gothling:	**exactly**
Ms.T:	e-dentities
gothling:	**whole new personalities. like costumes and masks and foreign accents. see, bliss?**
bliss4u:	oooo, i c now. this could be fun...
Ms.T:	yeah, i know just how to get to beau baby
gothling:	**oh, ahem. not so fast, sweetie**
bliss4u:	now what?
gothling:	**er, well, just that it won't be ms. tamra gray and beau baby.**
	it will be... <ta daa> BLISS and beau baby!
bliss4u:	excuse me?
gothling:	**as a different person, of course**
bliss4u:	what r u talking about?
Ms.T:	niiiiice. so bliss goes after beau, which leaves me available for... oh NO.
gothling:	**now ur gettin it**
bliss4u:	help!! I'M not gettin it
Ms.T:	what's not to get?
gothling:	**u trade boys u trade boys u trade boys**
bliss4u:	now i'm gettin it...

Ms.T:	this'll never work, annie
bliss4u:	i don't get it
gothling:	**of course it'll work**
bliss4u:	we trade boys?
Ms.T:	they'll never go for this
gothling:	**\<slamming forehead on desk once, twice, three times\>**
	ok listen up, campers. everybody take a deep breath
	here's the deal
	so, bliss's grandmother is sick and bliss needs 2 go help her. tamra, official best friend, gets 2 go along 2 keep her company
	u with me so far?
bliss4u:	but my grandmother is fine
Ms.T:	pretending...
gothling:	**what u really do is hole up at home 4 a couple of days. we'll be in chat mode constantly**
bliss4u:	yay! we could do a sleepover!
gothling:	**or not.... anywho, while ur "away," 2 very interesting chicks chat up yr boys online**
Ms.T:	kewl
gothling:	**lemme see. chessmaster mitch gets his king row invaded by... oh let's say Tatiana. yeah, Tatiana del Capo, some kind of genius gurl from italy— or no: albania**
bliss4u:	where's that?
gothling:	**and this tatiana chick is played by our very own tamra gray**

Ms.T:	gee thanks. Ta-tyahn-a from Al-bahn-ya. like a lady wrestler
bliss4u:	lol. i like it
gothling:	**mitch is smart, T. but u got world stuff in yr 47 AP classes, right? of course u did. everything is politics 2 u**
Ms.T:	i could look it up...
gothling:	**good. so then beau boy hears from a certain... Bridget... or Bonnie... or... lil help with the last name, tam**
Ms.T:	grindstaff, a banker's daughter from london
gothling:	**oooo, yes. and portrayed, of course, by the lovely and talented bliss taylor**
bliss4u:	i still don't get this. why me and beau?
Ms.T:	we trade boys... it's crueler that way. more like annie
gothling:	**it just keeps u... honest. ho ho**
Ms.T:	nice one, annie
bliss4u:	but me and the hottest boy in the state? i don't think so. u do it yrself, annie
gothling:	**don't make me come over there**
Ms.T:	come on, bliss, you can handle this
bliss4u:	but he's so... what would i SAY 2 him???
gothling:	**i'll tell u what 2 say**
Ms.T:	oh, you just go: beau, i am utterly muddled by what you americans call football, and you seem like just the chap who could help a poor english girl understand
gothling:	**perfect**

bliss4u:	hmmm. well, but we have 2 actually see them sooner or later
Ms.T:	true. annie?
gothling:	**not really. bridget and tatiana just have 2 set them up online**
bliss4u:	but...
gothling:	**we wing it, k? the point is, they agree to hook up, and then guess who appears?**
Ms.T:	bliss and tam, of course
bliss4u:	i don't know. this whole thing is kinda sketchy
gothling:	**what sketchy? it's a sting. like cops and a speed trap**
Ms.T:	spies and a politician
bliss4u:	but it's setting them up. how twisted is that?
gothlIng:	**law-abiding citizens have nothing 2 fear. don't u trust him?**
bliss4u:	oh puhleeeze. i trust mitchie completely
Ms.T:	i have a question. what are the stakes here? what do we lose if you win, annie?
gothling:	**oh, u lose plenty**
bliss4u:	come on. what does that mean?
gothling:	**yr innocence, for starters**
Ms.T:	annie thinks we're naive. <sigh> no faith, no faith
gothling:	**well duh**
bliss4u:	but why, annie?
gothling:	**o, just listen at u. "i trust mitchie completely."**
bliss4u:	well, i do. so there

gothling: **i rest my case. so there**

Ms.T: ok ok, so if we lose the bet, we lose our innocence and our faith in men. that's the best you can do?

gothling: **what? u want a money bet? make it 10 bucks. make it 20. i'll be rich**

bliss4u: yikes. 20??

gothling: **u don't want 2 bet money?**

Ms.T: no money. and we need a timeline. this isn't going on forever

gothling: **fine. how bout this: we scam them for 3 weeks. WHEN u lose, no matter how mad u are, u have to take them back, where u have to deal with their hurt little egos, knowing u'll never EVER trust them again**

bliss4u: yowtch

Ms.T: so dark, annie. tsk tsk... and what do we win when we prove you wrong?

gothling: **u say**

bliss4u: she has 2 kiss em both—like in middle school :-D

gothling: **whatever**

Ms.T: eww. no, she has to do something serious. like apologize

bliss4u: 2 us?

Ms.T: to them. she has to confess the whole thing and admit she was wrong about guys. the hardest thing in the world. especially for annie.

gothling: **have i mentioned my new black nail polish? not a chip anywhere**

Ms.T: girlfriend, these guys aren't like him

bliss4u: ...who must not be named...

gothling: **come on, campers. they're all like that. the ones who don't cheat r the ones who never got a chance. so do we have a deal or not?**

Ms.T: deal

gothling: **bliss? u in?**

bliss4u: annie, that is so not true about guys. mitch would never ever ever, and i'm sure he's had chances

Ms.T: really? i haven't noticed the cheer squad hitting on mitch...

bliss4u: very funny, my former friend

gothling: **seriously. when were all these chances 2 cheat?**

bliss4u: i don't know, k? i just know he would never do it

gothling: **then ur in, right? nothing 2 lose**

bliss4u: i'm thinking. there's something about this that is a little bit sick and wrong

gothling: **and yr point is?**

Ms.T: lol

gothling: **seriously, gurl. if u trust him, then where's the risk? it's just a game**

bliss4u: i know, but still

gothling: **plus, u get 2 know beau a LOT better : ->**

bliss4u: lol

Ms.T: hey, easy with that

gothling: **think of it as a chance for mitchie 2 PROVE that ur right about him**

bliss4u: hmm... well...

Ms.T:	come on, blissie. it'll be fun. like wearing costumes to the dance
gothling:	**a masked ball**
bliss4u:	yeah... i do like a costume
Ms.T:	a formal dress, a foreign accent, a shiny little mask on a stick
gothling:	**or cowgirl boots and a lone ranger mask**
Ms.T:	it'll be fun...
bliss4u:	yeah, it could be
gothling:	**so ur in?**
bliss4u:	ok ok, i'm in

CHAPTER 2
premonitions

THE DAWG HOUSE

MAY 27 08:15 PM

chessman has entered

chessman: bo. u there?

BoBoy: dude. sup?

chessman: nothing really. paper for history

BoBoy: no way. that's due tomorrow???

chessman: relax. it's not due till wednesday.
i'm just getting a head start. the
last paper of the year. ahhhh

BoBoy: mitch, u kill me, man. this is sunday night

chessman: i know. but see, if i'm done early,
then i have time to bail u out at the
last minute

BoBoy: lol. that's why i keep u on the payroll

chessman: so what did you guys do after
the game?

BoBoy: me and T? no mucho. a little smoocho.
winkwink, know what i mean?

chessman: go to the mall again?

BoBoy: lame, huh? <sigh>

chessman: not really

BoBoy: it is. i know it is

chessman: whatever dude

BoBoy: what can i say? i'm scared 2 put the big move on her

chessman: it'll happen when it's right. don't
let the team shine you about that

BoBoy: nah... they think it's impassive 2 be going out
with her at all

chessman: impassive?

BoBoy: u know, like: whoa, dawg, impassive touchdown!

chessman: oh. impressive

BoBoy: impressive! my bad. i knew that

chessman: close enough. well i'm just
checking in

BoBoy: hey. sometimes tamra's too much for me.
know what i mean?

chessman: too much?

BoBoy: nah. i mean, it's just like, what's she doing with me?
of all people?

chessman: i figure she likes you. why fight it?

BoBoy: i hear ya. but really, dawg, that girl has a brain on
her. she can think circles around me

chessman: ok, but you gotta ask yourself,
would she waste her time on a moron?

BoBoy: i guess not

chessman: seriously. besides, you're a
gentleman, which women always dig

BoBoy: true. well, what about johnson? he's no southern
gentleman

chessman: dude, get real

BoBoy: no u get real. he hooks up with tons of chicks

chessman: tons of skanks, you mean

BoBoy: true... still

chessman: you think johnson would ever, in his
wildest dreams, have a chance with T?

BoBoy: ha. not so much

chessman: exactly. so you, my man, have GOT
something

BoBoy: well... i gotta say yr logic is perfect, once again

chessman: that's why i'm the geek around here

BoBoy: my dad says for guys like us. there r 2 rules with
women—treat em like a lady, and make em laugh

chessman: guys like us?

BoBoy: me and him. u know, not the sharpest bricks in the
load

chessman: good advice. sharp isn't necessarily
what women look for

BoBoy: lol. if it was, my man, T would be with u

chessman: yikes. no way. too much pressure for me

BoBoy: pressure?

chessman: way too much. i would totally freeze
if i had to hook up with her

BoBoy: get out

chessman: no, she's impressive, but i like
her right where she is—with you.
at the mall

BoBoy: lol. u can just keep yr distance then. i'm not
complaining. but that is so weird, dude

chessman: why?

BoBoy: nah. i just mean she's nothing 2 fear, man. she's totally
not a competitive person

chessman: glad to hear it. i always liked her.
but take it from me, she kills in
AP classes

BoBoy: k sure, AND she totally imbues her politics

chessman: she what?

BoBoy: no, she totally does. but then she's got this happy little
way of hooking my arm around her. it cracks me up

chessman: i've seen her do that

BoBoy: like some kinda dance move, and boom,
she's tucked in tight

chessman: that's what i'm talking about.
she likes you

BoBoy: but hey. doesn't bliss do that kind of stuff?

chessman: bliss is great. really fine

BoBoy: she's awesome, dude

chessman: but she like, waits for me to move,
i guess. i dunno

BoBoy: yeah

chessman: i mean she's real cozy, but when we
go out, it's like, whatever you
wanna do, mitch

BoBoy: right. traditional girl

chessman: which is cool

BoBoy: it is

chessman: as long as what i want to do keeps her happy. :-)

BoBoy: lol. u worry about that?

chessman: definitely

BoBoy: so ur like—well, what do U wanna do?

chessman: yep

BoBoy: but that's cool. give and take

chessman: right

BoBoy: yeah.... i was saying 2 johnson... nah

chessman: what?

BoBoy: aw nothing. u know how he is

chessman: what did he say?

BoBoy: nah, he was just messing

chessman: come on...

BoBoy: nah, he was like, what does a hottie like bliss see in old mitch?

chessman: <snore> he says that stuff to me, too

BoBoy: i go, dude, the woman's in love. show some respect

chessman: i don't mind. johnson's cool

BoBoy: yeah

chessman: a little random, but he's cool

BoBoy: smart guy. jokes with all the teachers, but then he blows off classes. loves the women, but treats them like ho's... i dunno. hard 2 respect that stuff

chessman: witty, creative, sexist, underachiever. what's not to like?

BoBoy: lol. true. but he also calls u our nerdy friend

chessman: sure. but with capitals: Our
Nerdy Friend. like it's a title
or something

BoBoy: i don't like him talking that way. where's
his loyalty?

chessman: see, this is why Coach doesn't
start you. you don't want anyone
to get hurt

BoBoy: lol. u got me

chessman: it's fine about johnson. let it go

BoBoy: no it ISN'T fine. dude, he'll be lucky 2 graduate.
ur like on yr way 2 harvard and stuff

chessman: whatever

BoBoy: seriously. that is so far out of reach for anyone i know

chessman: no, it's cool. i AM your nerdy
friend. so what?

BoBoy: get out. but hey if it's cool with u, i'll let it alone.
i just think he should... i don't know

chessman: show some respect

BoBoy: something like that

chessman: nah. i'm just glad to hang with
you guys

BoBoy: hah. u have serious issues, dawg

chessman: you have no idea how boring it
gets in geek land

BoBoy: LOL. i know i'll never see harvard

chessman: stick with Ms. T

BoBoy: oh, i get it. good one

chessman: that girl is way smart. and she
does it without getting called
a nerd. gotta admire that

BoBoy: **bliss is no dummy either**

chessman: true true true. but... well...
bliss doesn't really live in her head

BoBoy: **like she should act smarter?**

chessman: nah, i just mean she really likes
her thing with the cheer squad and
all. she's smart about social stuff,
you know?

BoBoy: **u saying that's bogus?**

chessman: no, i totally like it. bliss is
popular. good for her. i'm just
not part of that crowd

BoBoy: **oic**

chessman: i'm her boyfriend and like this
third wheel at the same time

BoBoy: **no, i get it**

chessman: no you don't. you're one of the
popular gang. how could you get it?
;-)

BoBoy: **jocks and chicks. it's a beautiful thing**

chessman: lol. so it's like you say tam can
think circles around you. bliss can
TALK circles around me

BoBoy: **she does have lotsa friends...**

chessman: tell me. she's always calling
somebody, or texting somebody,
or just WITH somebody

BoBoy: **dude, ur jealous!**

chessman: nah. i'm just... ok, you got me,
i'm jealous

BoBoy: **i knew it. u tell bliss?**

chessman: nah, i don't complain

BoBoy: tell her, man

chessman: no way. i'm lucky just to be going
            out with her. i mean, look at me

BoBoy: true

chessman: lol. and btw? your history paper
            is toast

BoBoy: no really, i get ya. i'm totally insecure about
            the same thing

chessman: what? like someone's going to move
            in on you?

BoBoy: u know it

chessman: get out. Ms. T's too smart for that

BoBoy: no, i mean it. i get these prepositions

chessman: ??

BoBoy: when something's gonna happen...

chessman: oh, premonitions. sure. i get those

BoBoy: i'm like running scared half the time

chessman: really? so what's your premonition
            lately?

BoBoy: i don't know. she could change her mind, i guess

chessman: i hear you. there's always the chance

BoBoy: i guess

Big.J has entered

Big.J: yo. anybody home?

BoBoy: what up, J?

chessman: hey Johnson. how's it goin?

Big.J: omg, it's da both of dem. frick and
            frack doing their after school thang

chessman: i told you he was witty, didn't i?

Big.J: it's mickey and goofy. popeye and bluto. death and destruction. delight... AND instruction

BoBoy: he works on this stuff. gotta respect the discipline

Big.J: dudes, it is hard 2 believe, and i don't like 2 brag, but once again, i am the gingerbread on the smorgasbord of love

BoBoy: u what?

Big.J: smother me with lemon sauce and serve me sizzlin. yowza!

chessman: how do you do it, johnson? always the women

Big.J: ah, my poetic spirit. they cannot say me nay

BoBoy: get outta town

Big.J: one look into these soulful eyes, and their sugary pink hearts just melt 2 goo

chessman: it's a gift, bro. no 2 ways about it

BoBoy: LOL

Big.J: it's a gift... and a curse

BoBoy: what curse? u always have a lady at yr side

chessman: so do you, but with johnson it's a different lady every time

Big.J: yr friend has a brain on him, i c

BoBoy: so wattup today, J?

Big.J: what indeed? care 2 guess? anyone? anyone?

chessman: hmmm. love is on his mind, and...
           let's see, it's been...

BoBoy: **u met tiffany's mother and she's stolen u
           from tiff?**

Big.J: i'm thinking not

chessman: oh no. it's tiffany. she's lost
           that new car smell

Big.J: now, that's why u the king of the
           nerds. u figure things out....

BoBoy: **what r u saying, johnson? i've heard none of this**

chessman: ...plus there's a new car on the
           street

Big.J: check and mate. the chess dude
           wins again

BoBoy: **wait a minute. what happened to tiffany?**

Big.J: moving 2 woodstock as soon as
           school's out. her dad is changing
           companies. and i'm not driving up
           there every other day. that's 1
           thing...

BoBoy: **dude, that's a drag**

Big.J: u'd think. but somehow... i dunno.
           it wasn't going 2 work out with
           tiff anyway

chessman: something about the poetic soul
           getting restless?

Big.J: there u go. i need variety.
           i need stimulation. challenge.
           i have needs

BoBoy: **um, does tiff know?**

Big.J: know what?

chessman: about variety

BoBoy: **about yr needs, big J**

Big.J: she'll get the picture

chessman: what are you going to tell her?

Big.J: i'll think of something. she
texted me a minute ago. crying
about having 2 pack her stuffed
animals 2nite

BoBoy: **bro, that's cold**

Big.J: get a grip, dawg. i'm too young
to marry. and hey, i always let em
down gently. i'll write her a poem

chessman: it's a shame, though. tiff was the
best you've hooked up with so far

Big.J: if u don't mind a muffin top and
constant gum snapping

BoBoy: **get out**

Big.J: and cherry lipstick. but i rather
like cherry lipstick

chessman: come on J. she's who she is...

Big.J: she's a skank. u know that.
a sweet skank, but still

BoBoy: **aw man. where's yr heart? u keep it in a box
somewhere?**

chessman: well, um, nobody thought you'd be
with her long

Big.J: yo, check it out, my brothers. i'll
write her a poem right b4 yr eyes:
lets see, my image will be... k, a
bird. yes, a bird migrating. title?
anyone? no, i have it:

"farewell in spring"
for tiffany, on moving to
woodstock

my little bird, i know
that you must fly
—as birds in spring
are wont to do—and i
must set you free
to go where you must go
and be what you must be.

my little bird, i know
the universe
is calling you, and i
must be as strong
as i can be, and must not cry.
for though i long to fly
with you, my little bird,
and you to stay with me,
we know that I must let you
go.

my little bird, we
know the universe
is calling you
—as it, in spring
is wont to do—and i
must set you free.

that's it, dudes. what do u
think?

chessman: you've written this before

Big.J: no i haven't. i swear!

BoBoy: u just made this up?

Big.J: dude, this stuff just comes
2 me. i tell u, it's a gift

chessman: and a curse...

Big.J: lol. now ur a dead man. u don't
            mock an artist

BoBoy: dude, i don't know if it's good or bad, but u knock out
            a poem in 30 seconds and ur going to toss it at her
            like ttfn? shouldn't it cost u?

chessman: i think tiff would say it should, yes

Big.J: bro, that's just how it happens.
            i can't help it when the lightning
            strikes

BoBoy: u are truly cold, J

chessman: at least tell her to watch that
            screen door

BoBoy: really, johnson, she'll cry about this for a month

Big.J: boyz boyz, chill. hey, she's the
            1 leaving

chessman: and hey, easy come, easy go

Big.J: lay off, nerdman. she'll rebound
            in a week. i know this girl

chessman: no, it's cool. for the girls are
            calling you, and you must do what
            you must do

BoBoy: LOL, mitch. u guys crack me up

Big.J: look, very few guys can stay with
            1 chick forever. it isn't normal,
            man. play the field. hey, it's
            what they do

BoBoy: not me, dude. i'm totally staying with the 1 i got

chessman: it's what THEY do, johnson?

Big.J: zackly. every chick i know has
            had like 3 dudes this year. tiff

will find someone in woodstock,
and probably tomorrow

chessman: so, but let me just follow the
logic here. you think all women
are ho's, basically, is that
about it?

Big.J: u make it sound like a bad thing

chessman: ok, so they're all ho's. and that
makes you want to be one too? dude,
i hope that works out for you

Big.J: wellllll. looky here, looky here.
brittney's sending me a lil ol
text message on my lil ol cell
phone

BoBoy: oh, man. now brittney??

Big.J: i know. she's a ho. i'm weak.
i'm weak

chessman: and you must fly...

Big.J: btw, i will totally get u for
this. never mock a man's poetry.
an artist channels the universe.
if there's anything more important
than cherry lipstick, art would
be that thing

BoBoy: focus johnson! brittney on line 2, remember?

Big.J: k. i gotta bounce, dawgs.
check u 18r

CHAPTER 3
the setup

JUNE 01 04:15 PM

BoBoy has entered

BoBoy: yo mitch

chessman: hey

BoBoy: dude, what's this about bliss leaving?

chessman: ??

BoBoy: yeah. annie told me. she didn't say anything 2 u?

chessman: totally in the dark

BoBoy: dang. i saw annie, and she said something about B's mom or grandmom is vegetating

chessman: she what??

BoBoy: really sick in the hospital. like had a stroke or something

chessman: got it. but not her mom?
she's too young

BoBoy: mom or grandmom. she didn't know which.
just that B's gotta leave 4 a while. bummer

chessman: totally

BoBoy: so u haven't talked 2 B?

chessman: not since lunch. she had cheer
squad meeting, last day of school
stuff. then something with Tamra.
you know. she was going to IM me
later tonight

BoBoy: u better ask about this

chessman: absolutely. did annie say
how long?

BoBoy: she said it could be awhile. like months or longer

chessman: months? like all summer?

BoBoy: dude, i don't know. annie was just rattling
stuff off. she's like o it could be forever or it
could be just a weekend. all depends on the
hospital or something

chessman: where's the hospital?

BoBoy: tallahassee. i'm really sorry about this, bro

chessman: i'll check it out

BoBoy: dude, how can u be so chill? i'm freaked,
and it's not even my girlfriend

chessman: no, i'm plenty freaked. but i just
don't have enough information

BoBoy: i'm ballistic, man. i'm epileptic

chessman: lol. oh, wait. bliss checking in

✉ IM from bliss4u

JUNE 01 04:19 PM

bliss4u: mitch, honey, can we talk?

chessman: sure. hey, beau says there's something going on with your mom?

bliss4u: no, my grammy

chessman: what's happened?

bliss4u: i'm not sure. mom says she fell

chessman: did she have a stroke?

bliss4u: yeah. she totally freaked

chessman: no, your grandmother. did she have a stroke?

bliss4u: oh, right. i'm so dumb. no, she just fell. or, i mean, she could have... we don't know 4 sure yet. that could be it

chessman: that's a drag

bliss4u: i know

chessman: so what's going to happen?

THE DAWG HOUSE

BoBoy: **dude, what's she saying?**

chessman: it's her grandmother. she's fallen.
             maybe had a stroke

BoBoy: **i knew it. i knew it**

✉ IM from bliss4u

bliss4u: we have 2 go down there

chessman: you and your mom?

bliss4u: yeah

chessman: where is she? i mean where's the hospital?

bliss4u: oh, jacksonville. or no, it's lauderdale. silly. can't remember anything

chessman: wow, ft lauderdale's a long way

bliss4u: i know

chessman: why do you have to go?

bliss4u: um? cuz she's my grammy?

chessman: sorry. that was a selfish question. i just mean, if your mom is going, and all...

bliss4u: no, that's ok. i just have 2

chessman: i'll just miss you. totally

bliss4u: ur a sweetie. but don't worry, i'll come back

chessman: i'm not worried

bliss4u: mom needs my help with stuff

chessman: yeah...

bliss4u: like moving her back home, and helping her walk, and taking care of her, and yeah

THE DAWG HOUSE

BoBoy: oh man, i knew this was gonna happen. i knew something was gonna happen. it's my permutations. they been coming all the time lately. something's gonna happen. i knew it. this could be what they were telling me

mitch boy, what's she saying now?

chessman: she has to go down there to help her mom

BoBoy: dude

chessman: yeah

BoBoy: how long?

chessman: good point. i'll ask

📧 IM from bliss4u

chessman: does your mom say how long?

bliss4u: how long what?

chessman: how long you'll be there

bliss4u: oh. no she doesn't know 4 sure. it could be awhile, i think she said

chessman: what about cheer camp this summer? and then school? i mean, it's going to be our senior year

bliss4u: oh it won't be THAT long! school isn't till the end of August

chessman: eleven weeks

bliss4u: oh, silly, we'll be done with this in a week or 2. u'll see

chessman: really? beau made it sound like you're never coming back

bliss4u: beau? how would beau tanner know a thing about this?

chessman: from annie

bliss4u: yikes

chessman: and she was saying, like, indefinitely. maybe 3 weeks. maybe forever

bliss4u: well, k, maybe 3 weeks. but i don't think so. i don't think i could stand 2 do this that long

chessman: well, but it's your grandmother

bliss4u: sure. i know. um, but i just meant i couldn't do this 2 u. i told annie i didn't want 2 do it at all

THE DAWG HOUSE

BoBoy: i mean, u know how long it takes old people 2 get better. annie was like, it could be forever. that would be the worst, man. coming into your senior year and yr girlfriend like disappears

and who knows what she'd be doing all that time. those old boys in tallahassee know how 2 court a woman too. college town and everything

prepositions premonitions permutations. now i forget which 1 is right. dang. it's the stress

chessman: she thinks less than a month

BoBoy: dude. k. well, not as bad as it could be

chessman: not tallahassee. ft lauderdale

BoBoy: oh wait. here's T

chessman: see ya...

✉ IM from Ms.T

JUNE 01 4:30 PM

Ms.T: hey handsome, you there?

BoBoy: check it out, speak of the devil

Ms.T: whatcha doing?

BoBoy: thinking of u. what else?

Ms.T: lol. listen. we have to talk

BoBoy: totally. there's some weird stuff going on

✉ IM from bliss4u

chessman: so when do you have to leave?

bliss4u: i'm not sure what the plan is 4 that. i mean, it's up 2 my mom. she's the 1 driving and everything

chessman: you're driving to ft lauderdale? that'll take a while

bliss4u: or maybe we're flying. i can't remember. i am such a ditz today

chessman: well, you have a lot on your mind

✉ IM from Ms.T

Ms.T: there's something i have to tell you

BoBoy: sounds serious, T. fire away

Ms.T: don't mean to be that way. but it is kinda serious

BoBoy: i'm listening

Ms.T: well, bliss's grandmother has fallen down. it sounds like she might have had a stroke. they've put her in the hospital

BoBoy: hey, i've heard about this from annie. saw her after school

Ms.T: annie? she wasn't supposed to... well never mind

BoBoy: wasn't supposed 2 say anything?

Ms.T: sort of. anyway, it doesn't matter

✉ IM from bliss4u

chessman: but you think it could be soon? like this week you're leaving?

bliss4u: yes. oh. today. i'm just starting 2 pack

chessman: wow. that's quick

bliss4u: well, in a way. but who knows how long she'll last?

chessman: true. didn't think of that

✉ IM from Ms.T

BoBoy: when does she leave?

Ms.T: who?

BoBoy: bliss. 2 go help her granny

Ms.T: oh. right away. tonight

BoBoy: yeah. makes sense. gotta be there 4 those we love

Ms.T: yeah. has she told mitch?

BoBoy: um, yeah. he's chatting her right now. poor guy. this'll be rough on him

✉ IM from bliss4u

chessman: ok. but let's think positive. let's believe she'll be better soon, and THAT will help make it happen

bliss4u: o ur such a good guy

chessman: and you'll be back in no time

bliss4u: i really hate 2 do this 2 u

chessman: B, you're not doing it to me. you're helping your grandmother. that's important work. i know lots of people who wouldn't even go. she'll think you're an angel

bliss4u: ur right. it's important. still. i'm gonna miss u

chessman: and i think you're an angel too

bliss4u: i don't deserve u, mitchell saunders

chessman: but you'll call me or something?

bliss4u: i will. oh. um, grammy doesn't have internet

chessman: really?

bliss4u: but i'll call when i can

chessman: ok. wow. we've only been apart that one time

bliss4u: i know. 2 whole weeks away from u. and that jerk at disney world hitting on me. i hated it

✉ IM from Ms.T

Ms.T: bo, um, there's something else

BoBoy: what's that, miz T?

Ms.T: i need to tell you... how shall i put this?

BoBoy: oh no.... i know what ur gonna say

Ms.T: you do?

BoBoy: well, k... i'm guessing it's like... well, this isn't easy but maybe it's like...

so, now that school's over, u like want 2 see other people, don't u?

Ms.T: what? OMG no!

BoBoy: really?

Ms.T: REALLY. TRULY

BoBoy: whew. u were so serious

Ms.T: get that outta your head, bubba. you are totally stuck with me

BoBoy: T, that's such a relief. i was really sweatin there

Ms.T: what even made you think that?

BoBoy: dunno. just a hunch, i guess. i get these prepositions sometimes

Ms.T: well, that one totally steered you wrong

BoBoy: great. man, i was scared

Ms.T: really, beau. there's no man alive who could tempt me away. and don't you forget it

BoBoy: awww. i feel just like that about u, miz T

Ms.T: shucks

BoBoy: um... oh, dang it! it's not preposition, is it? :)

Ms.T: nope. ‹grin›

BoBoy: i knew it

✉ IM from bliss4u

chessman: i hated that guy too, and i wasn't even there. :-D

bliss4u: u had nothing 2 worry about

chessman: lucky for him... because i'd have come down there and... and given him a computer virus!

bliss4u: my hero <sigh>

chessman: hey, um, bliss? seriously?

bliss4u: yeah?

chessman: there aren't any guys down in ft lauderdale, are there?

bliss4u: ft lauderdale?

chessman: yeah. there aren't... oh never mind.
i was just thinking of something johnson said

bliss4u: johnson? mr. sleaze?

chessman: i know. he's a little sketchy... but

bliss4u: but what?

chessman: well, sometimes he thinks you're
nuts to be hooked up with a nerdster like me

bliss4u: listen, mitchie, i'm just an airhead cheerleader,
but i know what i've got in u

chessman: you're not an airhead

bliss4u: and i would never mess that up.
not in a million zillion years. u got that?

✉ IM from Ms.T

Ms.T: but listen, big sweetie

BoBoy: yes ma'am?

Ms.T: i have to go with bliss

BoBoy: say again?

Ms.T: when she goes to tallahassee

BoBoy: no way

Ms.T: way. i gotta go with her

BoBoy: i knew it. i knew something was coming

Ms.T: i know. you always do

✉ IM from bliss4u

chessman: so you're packing?

bliss4u: guess i better

chessman: this is so sudden. i'm going to miss you big time

bliss4u: don't worry, i'll be back b4 u know it. just...

chessman: what?

bliss4u: well, i know u

chessman: true

bliss4u: so i know this isn't a problem, but...

chessman: but what?

bliss4u: oh, just promise 2 be good while i'm gone, k?

chessman: lol. like the chess club girls are lining up. both of them

bliss4u: stop it. girls like u, mitchie. i hear them talking. ur smart and funny and wonderful. ur a real... oh what's my mom's word... a catch. ur a real catch. u just don't know it. and that's probably my fault. i should tell u more often

chessman: sweet. i can't wait to be mobbed at the mall. ;-)

bliss4u: i'm being serious, k? just shut up and promise

chessman: i promise. i swear. no messing around

bliss4u: good. better not

chessman: i would die first

bliss4u: well, let's not get carried away =)

chessman: you mean you'd miss me if I died?

bliss4u: hah. only at first. oh, my mom is yelling something

chessman: i'll swing by tonight to say bye, ok?

bliss4u: k. gotta run. luv u! miss me?

chessman: you too. i will. bye

📧 IM from Ms.T

BoBoy: k. i can deal with this. deep breaths, beau boy. take it easy big guy

Ms.T: you're too funny, you know? you always make me laugh

BoBoy: yessir. make em laugh, that's what my daddy says. but really, why do u have 2 go with her?

Ms.T: well, because i'm the best friend. that's what girls do

BoBoy: i was afraid of that. btw, it's lauderdale

Ms.T: what?

BoBoy: ft lauderdale. that's what she told mitch

Ms.T: no, it's supposed to be... well, never mind

BoBoy: what?

Ms.T: no, i could have remembered it wrong

BoBoy: no way. maybe she told u wrong

Ms.T: maybe

BoBoy: so r u packing right now?

Ms.T: yeah. listen, beau

BoBoy: tell me

Ms.T: you'll be good while i'm gone, won't you?

BoBoy: be good?

Ms.T: yes, duh. while i'm gone? get it??

BoBoy: oh that! oh man. trust me, miz T,
i'm yrs alone

Ms.T: {{bo}} you i trust. girls, i don't trust for
a minute. you're such a big handsome unit

BoBoy: u crack me up, girl

Ms.T: but don't evade the question. you promise me

BoBoy: i promise promise promise

Ms.T: once is fine. i trust you, but... well, thanks

BoBoy: no problem, lady. and hey, u gonna call me
or anything?

Ms.T: <sigh> i'll try, but her grandmother has like no internet, and we'll be at the hospital a lot, where you can't use a cell phone. and i don't know when we'll be free, you know?

BoBoy: drag

Ms.T: hey

BoBoy: what?

Ms.T: you're not worried about ME, are you?

BoBoy: nah. yeah. a little

Ms.T: beau honey, i promise you there's nothing like that to worry about. i'm trusting you, and you gotta trust me back. you put your premonitions to rest

BoBoy: can do, ma'am. that's what i needed 2 hear

Ms.T: :) you are really the find of the century, darlin. come say goodbye tonight, but i gotta run pack now. xoxo

BoBoy: k, T. i'll think of u all the time. xoxou2

THE DAWG HOUSE

BoBoy: dude, u still there?

chessman: still here

BoBoy: guess what T just told me. she's going with bliss

chessman: really? why?

BoBoy: girl stuff. best friend stuff

chessman: got it

ENTR@PMENT

BoBoy: u ok, dude?

chessman: i guess

BoBoy: i know. i'm totally bummed. ur thinking about what johnson said, aren't u?

chessman: not really. well, yeah. pretty much totally

i mean, i trust bliss. but i know what guys are like around her. makes me feel... i dunno. helpless

BoBoy: hey, hang in there. tam will be with her

chessman: yeah

BoBoy: and hey, not many guys to see in the hospital

chessman: true. i just can't believe how long it's going to be

BoBoy: a long road to hoe, but at least we're in the same boat on this

CHAPTER 4
a little help

 TXT to Johnson

June 02 02:30 pm
From: Gothling
IM me

 TXT to gothling

June 02 02:31 pm
From: Johnson
1 sec bz rt nw

TXT to Johnson

June 02 02:32 pm
From: Gothling
tk yr tm...

GURLGANG ROOM

JUNE 02 02:33 PM

Ms.T has entered

Ms.T: hey kids. sorry i'm late

bliss4u: where were u?

Ms.T: so i had to laugh. i'm innocently stocking up at the video store, cuz i don't want to be out while we're "gone."

i come out the aisle with an armload of dvds, and i nearly dump em all down mitch's back

gothling: **omg**

Ms.T: did a quick u-turn and ducked behind the dollar rentals. (how embarrassing)

bliss4u: what was he doing?

Ms.T: honey, he looked so bummed. he was flipping through the black-n-whites, just staring at the covers

bliss4u: that's my guy. he came over last nite 2 say goodbye, and i'm like, oh it's going 2 be so long, and he's all, i'm going 2 miss u so bad. it was sweet

Ms.T: i know. beau was a little panicky. like
         hyperventilating

gothling: **lol. he'll cope**

Ms.T: be nice, annie. you didn't talk to these
         boys

gothling: **i don't need their talk. i know their tiny black hearts.
         back shortly**

Ms.T: so bliss, did your mom see him?

bliss4u: she made me tell her the plan, or she
            wasn't going 2 disappear when he
            came by

Ms.T: yeah, well. bound to happen

bliss4u: mom was like why ARE u doing this 2
            poor mitch? don't u think he has feelings?
            stuff like that. she totally likes mitch

Ms.T: what did you say?

bliss4u: i blamed annie, of course >:)

Ms.T: lol

bliss4u: no really, i said oh it's just a test bla bla bla.
            so finally she said whatever, but if i lose
            mitch, she will definitely kill me

Ms.T: i know. i got the same thing

bliss4u: really?

Ms.T: mom just said "i won't lie for you." but my
         dad was totally pissed. "you're just playing
         him cause he's a white boy, aren't you?"
         no, daddy, no. "i thought i raised you better.
         yadda yadda." he thinks beau treats me
         really well.... which is true. <sigh>

bliss4u: <sigh>

TXT to Johnson

June 02 02:36 pm
From: Gothling
still WAITING

📨 IM from Big.J

JUNE 02 02:37 PM

Big.J: yo annie, wattup?

gothling: johnson, how dare u keep a lady waiting?

Big.J: annie, ma petite, so sorry. but i have another <ahem> lady on my screen at present

gothling: why am I not surprised? which skank is it this time?

Big.J: um, well... in fact, it's brittney. i think u know her. heh heh?

gothling: eww. brittney now???

Big.J: u don't care 4 brittney?

gothling: johnson, what is yr problem? ur not really a moron, so is it like a hormone imbalance, or what?

Big.J: can i get back 2 u on that?

gothling: whatever

Big.J: thx

gothling: hey, johnson. i have something going here, and i thought you might kick in. a lil help, u might say

Big.J: why would i EVER want 2 help u? inquiring hormones want 2 know

gothling: because it's evil

Big.J: ah yessss... our 1 weakness. please 2 tell us more

gothling: mitch and beau are going 2 be very lonely very soon

Big.J: so i hear

gothling: tam and bliss think the boys will be good while they're away

Big.J: it's possible

gothling: depending on who they meet in the meantime

Big.J: of course. so?

gothling: well... i have a couple of prospects 4 them

Big.J: already? no way!

gothling: yes way. so i need u 2 play a little puppet master with me

Big.J: puppet master! u sweet talker. hmm... and i do owe them a small payback

gothling: good

Big.J: but wait. who are these so-called prospects?

gothling: bliss and tam

Big.J: ummm...

gothling: surely u knew the whole gone-2-grandma's bit was a fiction?

Big.J: be still my heart

gothling: u really didn't know?

Big.J: nobody here suspected nuffin! ur a genius, gurl

gothling: true, true. still, if u missed it, things worked better than even i had hoped

Big.J: a compliment??? oh, u really MUST want something

gothling: shut up, J

Big.J: so... then the next step would be 2 bring the "prospects" onstage?

gothling: right

Big.J: but they can't appear in person, obviously. so that means... ah, invent characters 4 them online, yes?

gothling: correct. we're settling on names and personalities now

Big.J: excellent. this is really inventive, annie dearest. so we just need 2 get them chatting 2 the lonely boys club

gothling: i knew u'd find this amusing

Big.J: amusing? gurl if this works, it will be historic. and u know i don't exaggerate

gothling: never in a zillion yrs

Big.J: i may have 2 write an epic 4 u when this is over

gothling: if it's like what u wrote tiffany, we can just let it go

Big.J: shh, i'm scheming.... it happens that i owe the school some tech work this summer. this could work... yes, i may be able 2 help u

gothling: awesome. oh, um, btw... did i mention that my gurls r switching?

Big.J: not sure i see.... they switch?

gothling: think, my man. tamra takes the chessman as her pawn, and little bliss shakes the tree called big beau

Big.J: they switch!... omg. it's shakespeare. it's mozart! i'm all in a dither.... just get a load of yr bad self

gothling: flatterer

Big.J: oh cruella de ville, marry me this instant, i beg u, and end my misery

gothling: we'll see, we'll see. today i'm busy

Big.J: oops. 1 sec. brittney on line 1 again. heh heh...

gothling: ok, but make it snappy this time, jasper. we got schemes 2 scheme

GURLGANG ROOM

Ms.T:	i dunno, bliss, i may be feeling guilty... ish
bliss4u:	about this whole thing? totally

Ms.T:	but then, i dunno, it's also kinda fun
bliss4u:	bliss and tamra's excellent adventure
Ms.T:	it will be interesting for sure
bliss4u:	well, it will be fun 2 prove annie wrong =)
Ms.T:	sure. but i mean it's like a two-way mirror. i kinda want to see what beau will do when he thinks i'm not watching
bliss4u:	oh he won't do anything
Ms.T:	you're so sure?
bliss4u:	i just know he won't. besides, eww
Ms.T:	what?
bliss4u:	T, ur my best-est friend. how am i going 2 make a move on yr boyfriend?
Ms.T:	true. the yuck factor
bliss4u:	plus, we only win if he's a good boy, so why would i?
Ms.T:	to find out
bliss4u:	get real
Ms.T:	well, i guess i'd like to know for sure
bliss4u:	i won't do it, T
gothling:	**oh yes, u will**
bliss4u:	hi there, annie =)
gothling:	**yes u will make a move on beau boy, and u know why?**
bliss4u:	come on, annie. ur so serious all the time
gothling:	**because tam is going 2 find mitch totally, _totally_, fascinating**

Ms.T: now THAT was cruel, miss annie

gothling: **call me cruella, but prove me wrong**

✉ IM from Big.J

Big.J: k. i'm back

gothling: finally

Big.J: man, brittney is a whiner. her mom this, her sister that. why don't i come over? why don't i take her 2 the mall?

gothling: johnson, ur wasting yrself with her. u know that, right?

Big.J: i know, i know. she's temporary

gothling: it's pathetic, dude

Big.J: oh look, there she goes again. whatever

gothling: whatever. k, listen up. here's the plan

YOUR UNCLE JERRY'S BLOG

Masks and Mask-osity
03 JUNE

The mask is the face.
—Susan Sontag, lame old philosophy quote

Peace and joy. Lately, some campers have written Your Uncle Jerry to ask about avatars. Avatars. Are they more than pictures? When should you change them? Do they cause a twitch or rash? May you have more than one? Should you talk with your parents about them? So many questions.

In Your Uncle Jerry's dictionary, young camper, "avatar" comes right after "mask," which comes right after "face." Now, a mask is something You put on, to put on a new You. But a mask is not JUST for Halloween. Think of how many masks you wear in RL. You have a mask for home, a mask for school, a face you wear to Grandma's house, a face for that party at your friend's house. Those are avatars of you, dontcha see. Different incarnations, different sides of you. And sometimes you make one up online so you can be someone totally new.

On social sites such as the wasteland known as MySpace, camper girls and boys should *never* show their home faces; they should *always* don a different mask. "Yes, my parents work at the embassy. I spend most of my time in Paris."

But then the question is, who am I when I wear a mask? Am I still myself, or am I a new identity? Is a mask dishonest? This brings us to ---->

Your Uncle Jerry's Rules of Mask-osity

Rule 1. Your face is a mask.

Rule 2. A mask is your face.

Rule 3. There is no rule 3.

Rule 4. There is no point in trying to figure this out.

Can you wrap your head around this, camper? If you ever allowed the Real You to appear, we both know how that would look: a huge blob in a diaper, flopped in front of the tube, pounding gummy bears and pizza with four hands. In short, you'd be your little brother. To cover their shame at creating such a monster, your parents make you adopt an avatar called Good Manners. Are good manners dishonest? Yes. But won't you be glad when your brother learns them?

Peace and joy.

CHAPTER 5
lonely hearts club

THE DAWG HOUSE
JUNE 04 06:55 PM

BoBoy has entered

BoBoy: dawg, u there?

chessman: yo

BoBoy: spirits up, my man?

chessman: sure. not a prob. you?

BoBoy: u bet. shootin hoops all afternoon

chessman: helps to stay busy

BoBoy: shootin hoops till my hands are raw

chessman: lol

BoBoy: i mean, it's still the first weekend, but i totally
              cannot let it rest

chessman: yeah

BoBoy: i keep turning it over in my mind. maybe a week. maybe 2. maybe 6. maybe maybe maybe

chessman: yeah

BoBoy: how long's it been? like 3 days or something?

chessman: 46 hours

BoBoy: dude, i need a hobby

chessman: tomorrow coming soon. you got that thing set up?

BoBoy: with the lawn care guys. yep. how bout u?

chessman: starting wednesday

BoBoy: what was it again?

chessman: phone surveys

BoBoy: kewl. so u'll call at dinnertime and piss off my dad, right?

chessman: right

BoBoy: sweet. always a bright spot in the evening

Big.J has entered

Big.J: ding dong

chessman: johnson. word up

Big.J: word

BoBoy: dr. J! what brings u out of the contumelious dark this evening?

Big.J: listen, dudes and dudettes. (what he say? never mind.) a small proposition

chessman: contumelious?

BoBoy: my new word. i even looked it up

Big.J: i do hate 2 come 2 u in time
            of need. however...

chessman: kewl. what's it mean?

BoBoy: now THAT i don't know. i just know it's in the
            dictionary

Big.J: hellooooo? click-click-click.
            i called information, but i got
            the drug abuse hotline...

chessman: sorry dude. bo's wordsmithing tonight
            :-D

BoBoy: so, Big.J. u need something? like from us?
            hard 2 believe

Big.J: touching, isn't it? like best
            friends

BoBoy: exactly like that

Big.J: actually, no. i don't need
            anything like a favor. more like
            an exchange. both sides have
            something of value. a trade

chessman: i'll just go get my boots on

Big.J: u know what? is it better if i
            come back later? u girls seem 2
            be out of the mood right now

chessman: no, please. give us the pitch.
            this is great

Big.J: bubba?

BoBoy: present

Big.J: i was saying. ahem. we all have
            something of value. u have,
            well, a certain ability with
            the keyboard. plus u have
            evenings free

BoBoy: that's cold. evenings free. like we're not totally aware of that

chessman: true though...

Big.J: put it this way. the women r gone, the dawgs r restless, and u need something 2 keep u from prowling

chessman: fair enough. and you have?

Big.J: i have a small technology project related 2 my, um, "summer scholar" program

BoBoy: dude. u got summer school? i thought u were such a talent. poetry and all

Big.J: i am a fair student, but there was the small matter of afternoon absences during the month of may

chessman: oh yes: the Tiffany Era

Big.J: zackly

BoBoy: say no more

chessman: so this project is for a tech class?

Big.J: 4 the eminent dr. bartolo

BoBoy: the contumelious bartolo. why do they put the 90-yr-old dude in charge of tech?

chessman: everyone else has a life...

Big.J: he wants me 2 test a new program

BoBoy: hey, no fair. i wanna do that

Big.J: well, now's yr chance 2 do that. unfortunately, my project has 2 be school friendly and useful 2 other students

chessman: a website

Big.J: actually, a chat room

BoBoy: yeah. way easier

chessman: so, but useful to students? how lame
            is that?

Big.J: true. still, if it's gotta be lame,
            i wanna push it off a cliff

chessman: hyper-lame. nutrasweet

Big.J: u do catch on. i don't care what
            they say about u

BoBoy: what's our part of this?

Big.J: well, here's the thing. it will
            be a chat room 4 exchange students
            coming in the fall

chessman: exchange student, you mean. there's
            only one. but hey, you can't get
            lamer than a one-man chat room

Big.J: there are 2, actually. but dr.
            bartolo doesn't know that. i told
            him 4. he thinks i'm after like a
            citizenship award

BoBoy: are these dudes or chicks?

Big.J: why do u care? oic.

            no, they're 2 guys from albania or
            somewhere. don't worry about little
            bliss, little tamra. they will
            approve

chessman: so what's for us to do? as if i
            didn't know...

Big.J: oh hang on. here's brittney IM-ing
            me. tee hee. back soon

✉ IM from gothling

JUNE 04 07:17 PM

gothling: johnson

Big.J: yelloooow?

gothling: are u talking 2 them?

Big.J: trying 2, yes, and i need 2 get back. i told them u were brittney

gothling: wait. what are they saying? bliss and T are here

Big.J: they're nibbling

gothling: reel em in, dude

Big.J: listen, it's not that easy with guys

gothling: jeeze i hate a whiner

Big.J: i am not whining. i'm telling u that dudes are not as easy 2 persuade as chicks. u had the easy part. i'll get back 2 u in a minute. now let me do my work

gothling: oh, yeah, dudes r genius. they see right through things

Big.J: mitch actually is a smart 1. u can't rush him

gothling: he's a pansy. if u can't handle this job, i'll do it myself

Big.J: just u back off, girlfriend. we'll do this my way or i spill the beans—all of them

gothling: well, just DO it. they're only a couple of guys

Big.J: real men take finesse, darling.... as u would KNOW if u had ever DATED one!!

gothling: oh, johnson. ouch. i love it when ur rough. now will u GO??

Big.J: viper

gothling: toad

THE DAWG HOUSE

Big.J: k, i'm back. but u know what, nerd boy? forget it. if ur too busy these summer evenings, i'll get someone else

BoBoy: but 2 do what? just out of curiosity

chessman: to chat, i'm guessing. so johnson is free for brittney

Big.J: brittney does have needs

BoBoy: and yr other babes

Big.J: perhaps a summer love. who knows? a poet is much in request

chessman: have you started your poem for brittney?

Big.J: har har... k look. so there's this new thing on the school server. i'll do the setup and give u and the foreign dudes a sign-on. then we chat at set times every evening. u with me?

chessman: hypothetically, yes...

BoBoy: contumeliously

Big.J: in the off times, u can also
            email inside the same program,
            or chat, whatever. got it?

chessman: sure

BoBoy: **k**

Big.J: point is, it makes a transcript
            that i can dump 2 bartolo as my
            project. he doesn't care what's
            in it, as long as it looks like
            we're giving the exchange students
            a good impression of the school,
            the flag, and atlanta (pearl of
            the sovereign south)

            plus, i have 2 show him how 2
            run the software

BoBoy: **i still can't believe u have summer school**

Big.J: i'll ignore that

            anyway, i just thought that if i
            build the chat room, locate the
            players, and wake up bartolo once in
            a while, i would be doing my share

chessman: and in return for being good buddies
            about this, we get what?

Big.J: helloooo?? u fill yr lonely
            summer EVENINGS! u light up the
            dreary architecture of yr SOULS!
            u r 16 and WITHOUT WOMEN this
            summer, r u NOT??!!!

BoBoy: **but what's the catch?**

Big.J: u exhaust me

chessman: well, in fairness, there's usually
            a catch with you, johnson

Big.J: one sec. brittney again...

GURLGANG ROOM

Big.J has entered

gothling:	**yo johnson.** **still can't get them 2 take the bait, can u?**
Big.J:	almost there
Ms.T:	well, i guess we win
bliss4u:	great. that was quick
gothling:	**lol. i have plenty of tricks left**
Big.J:	ladies, PLEASE. a little faith
gothling:	**did they go 4 it?**
Big.J:	they will
gothling:	**ok. i'll take over from here**
Big.J:	WILL u chill out? they'll do it. trust me
Ms.T:	yeah. no rush, annie. let him take his time
gothling:	**what have u tried? threats? bribes?**
Big.J:	i'm using reverse psychology. surely u've heard of finesse, darling
gothling:	**only from u, johnson. and every time u write it,** **my screen goes a sickly green...**
Big.J:	witch
gothling:	**troll**
Big.J:	ogress. medusa... harpy

THE DAWG HOUSE

Big.J: dudes, i can see this isn't going 2 work. well, i tried

chessman: i'm pretty sure there's a catch, but i don't see it yet

Big.J: u make it so difficult. why? what have i done?

BoBoy: nah, we just shining u, dude

Big.J: there's no trust anymore. no trust and no respect

chessman: true true. but we might do it anyway

BoBoy: yeah, i think i'm in

chessman: any prepositions on this, beau?

BoBoy: no, it's good. i'm in

Big.J: no, no... please don't be impulsive. give it some thought

chessman: ok, johnson

Big.J: you're online 24/7, but this will mean opening 1 more window...

chessman: ok big J

Big.J: it will mean putting down yr book, typing a word or 2...

BoBoy: lol. u don't read, do u mitch?

chessman: only when i'm chatting johnson

BoBoy: rotfl

chessman: wouldn't want to waste my time completely

Big.J: that's fine. i'm used 2 disrespect
           from the nerd patrol. my poetry
           isn't up 2 his standards

BoBoy: so when will u set up the room, J?

Big.J: it's ready. i just have 2 email the
           exchange dudes

BoBoy: k, send us the sign-ons

Big.J: ur sure?

BoBoy: sure

chessman: yeah, why not?

BoBoy: just make this fun, k? i am feeling contumelious lately

Big.J: my man, u have no idea how much fun
           this will be

chessman: see, i hate it when he says stuff
           like that

Big.J: g2g dudes. ttfn

GURLGANG ROOM

bliss4u: i can't believe u have johnson in on this

gothling: why? johnson's our inside connection

bliss4u: because he's a sleazeball, maybe?

gothling: don't be such a prude

Ms.T: yeah, johnson's in. we need him

Big.J: yo check it out, annie dearest

gothling: johnson, did they bite?

Big.J: they are eager 2 meet with
            a pair of lovelies from a
            foreign land

bliss4u: no way

Big.J: we should have u ladies outta
            exile by wednesday

Ms.T: i can't believe it

gothling: told u...

Ms.T: told us what?

Big.J: that i could get them on board,
            i'm sure. <ahem ahem>

gothling: that men r all the same

Ms.T: agreeing to join a chat room isn't exactly
            messing around behind our backs

Big.J: all in good time, sugar

**gothling: whatever. we're set. good work, J.
            i knew u could do it**

Big.J: brrr. i get such shivers when
            u patronize

gothling: though it took u long enough

CHAPTER 6
foreign affairs

GURLGANG ROOM
JUNE 06 10:59 PM

Big.J has entered

Big.J: k, kids, ready 2 go?

gothling: **just waiting 4 u, johnson. ur 14 mins late**

Ms.T: where oh where could he have been?

Big.J: i have a life too, peanut

gothling: **no time 4 brittney stories. let's go**

Big.J: fine. the boyz r just signing
              on now. u go first tatiana, then
              bridget, then me

gothling: **don't forget i'm here if u need me, kids. bliss?**

bliss4u: present

gothling: **i'm here if u need me**

EXCHANGE STUDENT ROOM **UNION HIGH SCHOOL**
JUNE 06 11:00 PM

chessman has entered

BoBoy has entered

BoBoy: sup mitchie

chessman: just got here

BoBoy: albania, where's that?

chessman: by italy

BoBoy: u look it up?

chessman: nerd patrol

BoBoy: so these r italian dudes?

chessman: no. it's like halfway to greece.
            across the water. totally different
            but nearby

BoBoy: got it. like miami 2 cuba

chessman: sorta. whatever

Tatiana has entered

Tatiana: hallo?

BoBoy: union high chat room

Tatiana: excuse? me?

chessman: he said this is the union high school
            chat room. for exchange students

Tatiana: of atlanta, usa?

BoBoy: u got it

chessman: that's correct. this chat room is for exchange students at union high school

Tatiana: yes, that's who i am

BoBoy: **ur an exchange student?**

Tatiana: yes, for high school union. atlanta, usa

chessman: oic

Tatiana: sorry, what means "oic"?

BoBoy: **means he understands now**

chessman: it means "oh, i see." american slang

Tatiana: oic

BoBoy: **right**

Bridget has entered

Bridget: hello, good morning

BoBoy: **union high chat room**

chessman: this is a chat room for exchange students at union high school in atlanta

Bridget: brilliant... everything worked. hello, everyone. i'm bridget

BoBoy: **so, ur like an exchange student, too?**

Bridget: very much like 1

Big.J has entered

Big. J: yo, group, it's me. everyone here yet?

BoBoy: **sup J**

Tatiana: hallo, johnson

chessman: been looking for you...

Bridget: hello, good morning

Big.J: good good good. so everyone's
               already getting 2 know each other.
               have we done introductions?

chessman: not as such. but i have a question
               for you

Big.J: hold that thought, mitchie.
               let's do intros. i'll go first

               my name is johnson. i'm the 1 who
               brought u all together. i've set
               up the chat room, and i'll be
               logging the chat for my summer
               educational project.

               who's next?

Tatiana: yes, i will be next. my name is tatiana
               del capo. i am living since many years in
               tirana, albania. it is beautiful mountainous
               country on adriatic coast

BoBoy: **adriatic? mitch said it was by italy**

chessman: the adriatic sea is between italy
               and albania

Tatiana: ah, you know of my beautiful country?

chessman: a little. i looked it up

               i'm mitch, by the way. mitchell
               saunders. i go to school at union
               high in atlanta, and i used to be
               a friend of johnson's

BoBoy: **beau tanner. i need to speak 2 johnson too**

Bridget: so. well. my turn, then. hello, good morning, i will be
               coming 2 atlanta as an exchange student from london.
               my name is bonnie grindstaff

BoBoy: bridget, u mean

Bridget: beg pardon?

⇶ IM from chessman

JUNE 06 11:06 PM

chessman: johnson, what gives?

Big.J: hello, good morning

chessman: these aren't guys, johnson. you said they'd be guys but they're chicks

Big.J: wait a minute. ur saying i knew? that i deliberately put u in a chat room with foreign women?

chessman: sure looks like it, J

Big.J: dude, chill. i just found out this morning when i emailed them

chessman: gimme a break

Big.J: go ask the office. the names they gave me were Bret and... something else. sounded like dudes 2 me. i only found out their real names an hour ago.

chessman: i don't think i can do this

Big.J: ur complaining?

chessman: i just wouldn't feel right. i promised bliss

Big.J: u promised her not to mess around. u didn't promise 2 sleep through the summer. besides, these chicks r overseas, dude. where's the danger?

chessman: we'll see...

BoBoy: u said bonnie just now, but yr name is really bridget, right?

Bridget: is it?

i mean, did i? oic. yes i surely did. i'm such a dunce. my little nephew calls me aunt bonnie. just learning 2 talk, u know

chessman: that's funny. i have a little niece who calls me uncle mick

Bridget: u do not

chessman: seriously. it happens with names. speaking of which, there was this thing about your name at union high school

Bridget: my name?

chessman: yes, funny thing. they have you with a boy's name on your record

GURLGANG ROOM

Big.J: bliss, quick, tell him u go by bret

bliss4u: what?

gothling: what happened?

Big.J: mitch is suspicious

gothling: **bliss, no, just say the letters have been coming 2 u as Bret**

Big.J: yes, better. and say "how dreary"

bliss4u: what r u guys talking about???

Big.J: quick!

EXCHANGE STUDENT ROOM **UNION HIGH SCHOOL**

Bridget: oh, that. how dreary. all the papers from atlanta have been addressed 2 bret grindstaff. like they lost 3 letters in my name

BoBoy: **no way. bret? like bret the guy's name?**

Bridget: i guess

Big.J: well, THAT certainly solves a mystery

BoBoy: **i like that word. dreary. how dreary**

Tatiana: i am feel very interested to be hearing this. since the first letter from atlanta, they are calling me as tim. does anyone know what means tim?

GURLGANG ROOM

Big.J: beautiful catch, tamra. very nice... love the accent, too

Ms.T: the accent sounds russian to me. gotta work on it

gothling: **russian, albanian, transylvanian, it's all good**

chessman: in english tim is a short name
for timothy. strange, though. it's
not even close to tatiana

Tatiana: oic. well, starts with T. includes I.
when does school office get everything
correct?

chessman: true...

Tatiana: you should see italian bureaucracy.
i am saying oic correctly, mitchell?

chessman: absolutely. and please call me
mitch

BoBoy: **but ur from albany, right? not italy**

Tatiana: albania. my mother, she is of italy.
so from a child i can speak the italian
and also the albanian

chessman: and the english

Tatiana: also the english. is true. but only those
three. i no have greek or serbian. not
a good language student, sorry

Big.J: this is fascinating, i must
say. so few americans know any
language besides english. heh heh.
and the english don't even think
we can speak that 1. right,
bridget?

Bridget: i have a question about names

Big.J: right, bridget??

GURLGANG ROOM

bliss4u: annie, i don't like this

gothling: what??

bliss4u: johnson is too bossy

Big.J: oh, puhleeeze.

Ms.T: come on, bliss! play along. you're doing great

Big.J: i'm only trying 2 get us off the name thing. ur gonna blow the whole game

EXCHANGE STUDENT ROOM **UNION HIGH SCHOOL**

Bridget: i was just sitting at my desk here in london, u know, and i wondered why they call u Johnson. don't u have a proper 1st name?

Big.J: oh dear. proper first name. so english. oh my

BoBoy: lol. well, see, the thing with johnson is that his mother couldn't think of a name 4 him

chessman: he was too ugly

BoBoy: they didn't have a baby name that ugly

Big.J: ignore them, ladies. american humor is so shallow

chessman: he was so ugly that when he was born...

BoBoy: the doctor slapped his dad

Bridget: rotfl. nice 1, beau

BoBoy: thank yew. thank yew very mush <hand to heart>

Tatiana: a good team, if i am understanding this joke

Big.J: ah, we're all so giddy tonight. what fun we're having in america

---

✉ IM from gothling

gothling: johnson, how goes it?

Big.J: i hate these people. hate em

gothling: r they teasin u, baby?

Big.J: morons! if they knew what i know...

gothling: let it go, wuss

Big.J: wuss?! now ur turning on me too?

gothling: u can take it, johnson. grow up

Big.J: arrrrgh... i hate it when ur right

gothling: get used 2 it

Big.J: if u weren't so evil, i'd hate u too

gothling: they'll get theirs

EXCHANGE STUDENT ROOM **UNION HIGH SCHOOL**

Bridget: slapped his dad. i just love american humour

chessman: seriously? i've always liked british

Tatiana: is very dry, the english humore

chessman: exactly. more satire, more absurd

Bridget: maybe. i like the 3 stooges, myself

BoBoy: the stooges rule! and tom & jerry

Tatiana: mitchell saunders, please to tell me
                what your town atlanta is in august.
                am i to wear the warm clothing?

Bridget: i love tom & jerry!

chessman: very hot in august. you do not
                want warm clothing

BoBoy: on guard, monsieur pussycat!

Tatiana: so somethings cooler. understood

chessman: in fact, most of us go naked in
                august

Bridget: u do not!

BoBoy: lol. well, mitch does, but u wouldn't wanna see it ;-)

Tatiana: who knows? perhaps i would join him. <a
                joking>

Bridget: and what do u wear in the summer, beau?

BoBoy: aw man. by august i'm in pads and practice jersey

chessman: beau is a football player. this year
                he may even make second string

Tatiana: i am sure he is very fine player

**BoBoy: mitchie's teasing me, but he's right. i'm not hard
                core enuf 2 be any good**

Bridget: beau, sometime maybe u would explain the game
                u americans call football. i get all muzzled

BoBoy: muzzled?

Bridget: puddled

chessman: lol

Tatiana: muddled, i am sure she means!

Bridget: right, sorry. it muddles me, rather. know what i mean, guv?

BoBoy: hey no prob. yeah, i can teach u that stuff easy

chessman: wait... "it muddles me, rather." i've read that somewhere

BoBoy: i mean, i can tell u the basics

chessman: are you sure you're from england?

Tatiana: mitchell, what in your spare time do you do on summer?

Bridget: of course i am. but me mum is irish a little. a wee bit of the irish there

Big.J: well, group. i said that this would be a short session since i know that tim and bret—i mean tatiana and bridget—have 2 be going. the day starts early on the other side of the ocean...

Tatiana: is very true. i have almost 7 of the clock now. in the morning

Bridget: o my yes. look at the time

BoBoy: well, hey. u'll check in again tonight, right?

chessman: tomorrow

BoBoy: doh. tomorrow morning

Bridget: oh, i was thinking the same thing. i'm such a ditz

BoBoy: a ditz? they say ditz in england? kewl

Tatiana: the american television is in everywhere, my friend

Big.J: listen, we'll meet at the same time every day. but u can chat each other lots in between. this server runs 24/7, and school wants us 2 be best friends by the end of summer. heh heh

chessman: see bro, there he goes again...

Big.J has left the room

BoBoy: what?

Bridget: well. good nite. or good morning...

Tatiana: ciao to everyones. very nice to have meeting you, mitchell

chessman: tell ya later

BoBoy: prepositions?

Bridget: cheers cheers

Bridget has left the room

BoBoy: cheers, bridge

Tatiana: goodbyes, mitchell?

chessman: right. cya later

Tatiana: cya?

chessman: sorry. see you later.

Tatiana: oic! goodbye for now

Tatiana has left the room

CHAPTER 7
facing the alter ego

gothling: **so, ladies?**

bliss4u: brrrr...

Ms.T: mitch is onto us

gothling: **don't be paranoid. johnson sent me the transcript and u done gr8!**

bliss4u: i was so nervous!!

Ms.T: i think he knows something

gothling: **johnson will take care of it**

bliss4u: but i thought i made a pretty good english girl...

gothling: **u killed, girlfriend**

Ms.T:	i about wet my pants when mitch said there's this thing about your name
gothling:	**who cares? it was johnson he didn't trust. u 2 were in the clear**
bliss4u:	i hate johnson
gothling:	**we need johnson**
bliss4u:	i don't like johnson telling me what 2 do
gothling:	**i'll talk 2 him**
Ms.T:	mitch knows he was lying
gothling:	**come on. u should be flattered**
Ms.T:	why flattered?
gothling:	**duh. johnson told them u were dudes because THEY didn't want to chat up foreign WOMEN**
bliss4u:	<sigh> true love
Ms.T:	still, mitch is dangerous
gothling:	**get a grip, T. the point is, u guys did great**
bliss4u:	how dreary. beau thought that was cute. i have to remember that. i'll make a list
Ms.T:	can johnson really handle mitch? can i even handle mitch?
gothling:	**it's fine. jeeze, u worry so much**
bliss4u:	cheers. i thought of that 1 myself. and spelling humor like humour
Ms.T:	you did great bridget. i mean bliss
bliss4u:	lol. u think so?
Ms.T:	yes i do. just don't get too attached to my man ;-)

bliss4u:	beau? please, i'm just playing him...
gothling:	**break his heart, girl**
Ms.T:	hey!
bliss4u:	i'm a player =)
gothling:	**tam, u were awesome with yr tatiana accent**
Ms.T:	these accent? oh, is nothing
bliss4u:	u were like, i dunno, a different person totally
Ms.T:	i kinda FELT like a different person
bliss4u:	it's funny, isn't it? i did too
Ms.T:	like i didn't know those guys at all
bliss4u:	i could say stuff as bridget that i would never say in RL
Ms.T:	yeah, like you would never stare down johnson in real life
bliss4u:	don't u have a proper name? i don't know what made me say it
Ms.T:	except he's so crude with his name
gothling:	**u took a big risk doing that, bliss**
bliss4u:	i know i did
gothling:	**if u slipped and let on that u know johnson...**
bliss4u:	i dunno. if it had been me taking the risk, it would have blown up in my face. but it was like not me
Ms.T:	like bridget was doing it
bliss4u:	there was just this other voice in my head
Ms.T:	me too. i like opened a room somewhere, and there was tatiana talking away in a foreign accent

gothling: <snore>

Ms.T: what?

gothling: u campers need 2 get a grip. haven't u done this before?

bliss4u: done what?

gothling: u know. worn a mask online. had a different e-dentity

Ms.T: have you?

gothling: all the time

bliss4u: oh right. like when?

gothling: like ur talking to uncle jerry clarkson of bloomington minnesota

Ms.T: you have a guy avatar? you made up a whole life for him and everything?

bliss4u: why would u do that? ewww...

gothling: oh u have 2. especially on myspace if ur a female. so many losers hitting on u

bliss4u: i know. that's why i quit going

Ms.T: so who's jerry clarkson?

gothling: u can call me Uncle Jerry—camp counselor, online preacher, amateur psychic, and broom-straw philosopher

bliss4u: how do u think this stuff up?

Ms.T: psychic? cool

gothling: totally. he reads tarot cards

Ms.T: what?? you like tell people they'll inherit a fortune or meet a dark man with a family message?

bliss4u: u really love 2 mess with heads, don't u?

gothling: no, it's kewl. jerry wouldn't hurt anybody

Ms.T: jerry wouldn't. annie would ;-)

gothling: heh heh heh

bliss4u: but really. tarot cards and boy scouts?
that doesn't go

Ms.T: so annie, read my cards, ok?

bliss4u: eww. no!

gothling: u don't need it, girl. tatiana needs it.
she's the 1 courting disaster

Ms.T: nah. she's only courting mitch

bliss4u: if she catches him, it will be a disaster
4 u. i'm serious

Ms.T: hey, you're after my beau boy. i gotta
defend myself

bliss4u: i am not after beau

gothling: no, dear, but bridget is...

bliss4u: get real

gothling: "there was this other voice in my head"

bliss4u: that doesn't mean...

gothling: "it wasn't me taking the risk... it was bridget"

bliss4u: that doesn't mean i would do anything

Ms.T: play nice, annie

gothling: i'm just saying u never know what yr alter
ego will do

Ms.T: ok, we get it

bliss4u: do u think that's so true?

gothling: totally. u never know. just like 2nite

bliss4u:	i think we were still in control
Ms.T:	well, but we were improvising like mad
bliss4u:	i just know i didn't say anything i'd regret later
gothling:	**not yet, but u will**
Ms.T:	don't listen, bliss. annie's in a dark phase this year
bliss4u:	she totally is
gothling:	**i just want our bliss 2 be clear on what she's doing and what could happen**
bliss4u:	like what?? i can bail anytime if i don't like how things r going. u can play yr little game all by yrself
gothling:	**don't u believe it. ur in this 2 deep 2 bail on me**
bliss4u:	i'll bail if i want 2. i swear i will
Ms.T:	kids, kids. let's not argue
gothling:	**really, bliss? did yr grandma get well all of a sudden?**
bliss4u:	maybe
gothling:	**because that's going 2 look fishy 2 mitch**
bliss4u:	so?
gothling:	**so he'll want a real explanation, and i happen to have 1**
bliss4u:	u wouldn't
gothling:	**yes, sweetie, i would. and johnson would back me up**
bliss4u:	mitch wouldn't believe johnson
gothling:	**the question is, can mitch believe u after this?**

Ms.T: come on ladies...

gothling: i don't even have 2 make up a story. u lied about yr grandma. u cried false goodbye tears. and u came back as bridget 2 hit on his best friend. how can he trust u now?

Ms.T: ok annie, you've made your point

bliss4u: ur truly an awful person, annie

gothling: ur too, but i still luv u...

so here's the thing: nobody bails until we see who wins the bet

Ms.T: come on. bliss won't bail. she was just talking. it's late and we're tired

bliss4u: rude, hateful, and mean-spirited

bliss4u is off-line

gothling: oh, fine. <sigh> she has no staying power in a fight

Ms.T: you cannot be rough with her, annie

gothling: she's a wuss

Ms.T: you play it too dark

gothling: she'll be fine

Ms.T: listen, if you break with bliss, then everything comes apart

gothling: whatever. it's her own throat she's cutting

Ms.T: you think she's weak, but she'll surprise you. and—just so you know—i won't take your side

gothling: okokok, i'll fix it tomorrow. jeeze

Ms.T: just remember you like this game more than anyone else does

CHAPTER 8
like a rock

THE DAWG HOUSE

JUNE 07 05:30 PM

BoBoy has entered

BoBoy: so dude. chat room 2nite?

chessman: i guess

BoBoy: u not sure?

chessman: no, it's cool

BoBoy: kewl

chessman: yeah. hey, you like them?

BoBoy: bridget and...

chessman: tatiana

BoBoy: right. she's harder 2 understand.

chessman: well, non-english

BoBoy:	yeah. albany
chessman:	albania
BoBoy:	really? oh, right
chessman:	bridget was a little... i dunno
BoBoy:	what?
chessman:	i dunno. kind of not so bright, i guess
BoBoy:	she was nice tho
chessman:	definitely. i'm just saying
BoBoy:	yeah
chessman:	yeah
BoBoy:	u like tatiana better?
chessman:	a little. why?
BoBoy:	no reason... but, well, would u like take her out or anything?
chessman:	get real. we just IM'd a little. besides —> bliss
BoBoy:	i know. i'm just sayin
chessman:	sure
BoBoy:	yeah

Big.J has entered

Big.J:	dawgs and dawgies!
BoBoy:	wazzup, J?
chessman:	zup
Big.J:	just passing on a message.
	i saw annie at the mall, and she talked 2 bliss last nite

chessman: cool

Big.J: yes. btw... something about phones.

chessman: um... mine is temporarily out of service

BoBoy: **dude. u run up the phone bill again?**

chessman: bliss likes to text. what can i say?

Big.J: whatever. bliss doesn't have her
           phone. she called from granny's
           landline

BoBoy: **no way**

Big.J: that's what annie sez

chessman: what about Ms. T?

Big.J: same same

BoBoy: **left her phone? oh like i believe that**

chessman: hmm

Big.J: well, that's the story... anywho,
           a message: more bad news 4 youse

chessman: what's that?

Big.J: another 2 weeks in tallyhussy

BoBoy: **another... man, i need a hobby**

chessman: okay. tell her i'll write. oh wait.
           i don't have the address. i'll call
           from somewhere. does annie have the
           phone number?

Big.J: never fear. i'll give annie a
           message of love and mournfulness.
           ur pining. ur wasting away. i'll
           take care of it

chessman: gosh, johnson, what a pal

BoBoy: **lol**

Big.J: on the upside, the chat room
            is doing very well

BoBoy: **it's flowering**

Big.J: u know, mitch, between us, i don't
            get half of what our bro says

chessman: it's flourishing

BoBoy: **see? no worries. mitch can translate**

Big.J: so i was saying. chat room again
            2nite, dudes?

BoBoy: **we're there**

Big.J: what do u think of the
            euro-hotties, eh?

chessman: what do you mean?

Big.J: nice ladies?

BoBoy: **yeah, nice**

chessman: whatever

Big.J: u should really lighten up,
            mitch boy

chessman: how is brittney, johnson? started
            your farewell poem yet?

Big.J: brittney is... well, 2 be honest,
            brittney is needier than i expected

chessman: ahhh

BoBoy: **Big.J, say it ain't so**

Big.J: alas and alack, tis true,
            i greatly fear

BoBoy: **alack?? what's that mean?**

chessman: same as alas. our Big.J is a
            literate man

BoBoy: well, i knew that

Big.J: gentlemen, u flatter me

BoBoy: i mean, goes 2 the opera and everything
<smirk>

chessman: and look at his poetry...

Big.J: okok, ahem, i was saying

chessman: and all that summer school

Big.J: the search 4 knowledge, my brother,
does not end with the school year.
nay, the quest goes on unto the
edge of doom, or at least till
june 19

BoBoy: lol. dawg, i can't keep up

chessman: so J. any news on the summer love
front?

Big.J: 4 lil ol me? perhaps...

BoBoy: perhaps. see, mitch, u gotta love a dude who
can say perhaps

chessman: perhaps one of the euro-girls?

Big.J: dude, no. those women r spoken 4

chessman: how do you know?

Big.J: ur kidding, right? right?

BoBoy: mitch, what's he talking about?

Big.J: get out. u didn't feel it?
don't tell me u didn't feel it.

chessman: what i felt was you trying to
pull something

Big.J: me? dude, ur totally up in
the night

chessman: i don't think so. i've got this
preposition

Big.J: ?? now it's mitch with the word
disease. i'm worried

BoBoy: **he means permutation. no, wait...**

Big.J: seriously, dawgs. u need 2
cut loose. u've been away from
yr women too long

BoBoy: **dude, that's the truth**

chessman: another 2 weeks now

Big.J: well, i don't know everything,
but i can tell u what works 4 me

BoBoy: **what's that, J?**

Big.J: love the 1 ur with

chessman: predictable, really

Big.J: hey those foreign ladies r coming
in the fall, and all u need 2 do is
cultivate them a little now

BoBoy: **cultivated. now there's a word**

chessman: like opera, like farming

Big.J: don't start on opera

BoBoy: **lol**

Big.J: serious, they'd be soooo grateful 2
have a friend they can trust
in a strange land

chessman: johnson, you don't seem to get this:
i am not available

BoBoy: **me neither. i'm a rock 4 ms.T**

Big.J: gimme a break. ur dying here

BoBoy: mitch is a rock 2

Big.J: yes, ur both COME SCOGLIO

BoBoy: we're what?

Big.J: co-may sco-lio, dude. like a rock. ur straight outta "cosi fan tutte"

BoBoy: kewl

chessman: what's your stake in this, johnson?

Big.J: \<sigh\> dude. it's nothing 2 me. have it yr way

BoBoy: or wait. mitch is a rock—i'm a brick

Big.J: i'm just saying u 2 r wrapped a little tight these days

chessman: ok. and i'm just saying bliss and i have an understanding

Big.J: no, that's cool. so she understands u and u understand her

chessman: something like that

BoBoy: it's a cultivated understanding

Big.J: why is there always 30 seconds of silence after he writes anything?

chessman: lol

BoBoy: what i say?

chessman: i'm still working that out, bro. but i think it was profound

Big.J: here's a thought. suppose u heard something that made u doubt yr faraway ladies?

BoBoy: u got something on bliss and tamra, dude?

chessman: no, he doesn't have anything

Big.J: just suppose i did

chessman: whatever

BoBoy: doesn't matter. i wouldn't listen

chessman: ok, so, hypothetically. what kind
             of thing would it be?

Big.J: what would make u doubt her?

BoBoy: like the worst that could happen?

chessman: seems obvious what that would be

Big.J: going out with another dude,
             right?

BoBoy: i'm gonna lateral this 1 2 mitch

chessman: going out with Big.J

BoBoy: rotfl <high 5s all around>

Big.J: well. i can c u boys r hard core

BoBoy: i'm a rock. what can i say?

Big.J: i'll just tell tatiana and bridget
             2 forget it

chessman: forget what?

Big.J: forget any ideas they might have
             had about cultivating dudes in
             atlanta. unless... well, sure. i
             can always dig up some other guys

BoBoy: get real

chessman: johnson, don't try and play us, ok?

**BoBoy: besides, those women have their own dudes back
             in albany. euro-dudes**

Big.J: sure they do

chessman: albania

Big.J: but look. they're going 2 be
           away from home, in a strange
           country. the euro-dudes will be far
           far away 4 a long long time

chessman: what's your point?

Big.J: they're in the same place u r
           right now. the point is simple
           friendship. online companionship.
           perhaps a trifle more

BoBoy: perhaps a summer online love

Big.J: perhaps. and seriously, why not?

chessman: don't even, beau. T would cut
           you into dog meat

Big.J: perhaps she would

BoBoy: no, she would definitely

Big.J: perhaps it would be worth it

CHAPTER 9
peach

Tatiana has entered

Tatiana: hallo mitchell? no one else is here?

chessman: hi, tatiana. just me, so far

Tatiana: mitchell, is good to see you

chessman: lol

Tatiana: i mean read you. well, what does one say for this in english?

chessman: no, it's cool. just funny, because no one can actually see online

Tatiana: yes, i understand. however, i would like to see you :)

chessman: um. yeah. hey, you know that joke about the dog?

Tatiana: a joke?

chessman: yes. 2 dogs at the keyboard. one says to the other: on the internet, nobody knows you're a dog

Tatiana: lol. is very true joke!

chessman: yeah, i like it

Tatiana: you have a good humore sense, i think

chessman: thanks

Tatiana: but excuse. how do i know you are who you say? lol?

chessman: nice one. how do i know your name is tatiana?

Tatiana: yes! ha, because i might be a dog!

chessman: :-) no, i don't think you could be a dog

Tatiana: well, you must to wait and see when i come to atlanta usa, no?

chessman: um, well, in albania, what would you say for "good to see you" online?

Tatiana: ah, in albania, one doesn't have the internet so much

chessman: oh right. not a wealthy country, i hear

Tatiana: is true. i am being very lucky because of this exchange with the america school

chessman: well...

Tatiana: mitchell, you have read something of my country, yes?

chessman: sure. i mean, well, just a little. i looked you up online

Tatiana: you are very sweet to do this

chessman: not really

Tatiana: sweet is correct, is it no?

chessman: um, yes, that would be correct. nice is another way to say it

Tatiana: no i am think sweet is what i mean

chessman: ok...

Tatiana: you make me feel important to read of my country, mitchell. usa is such important nation. for you to look up me online is great compliment

chessman: well i'm sure albania is important in many ways

Tatiana: we have very rich history but also much sorrow. a crossroads of empires. is correct, crossroads? where roads do cross?

chessman: yes correct. what are the people like in albania?

Tatiana: ah, we are a passionate people. passion is in the water, i think. lol

chessman: i see

Tatiana: especially the women are so very full of passion. the men are brilliant and handsome but they go to other country for working

chessman: i read about that

Tatiana: about our passionate women, lol?

chessman: um, about the men looking for work
in western europe

Tatiana: you are also brilliant and handsome, mitchell,
i think?

chessman: lol. actually beau is the brilliant
and handsome one

Tatiana: except he cannot remember the name of
my country. albany, he calls it

chessman: well, that's a point. but i remind
him

Tatiana: thank you, my friend. a very sweet thing
for to do

chessman: nah

Tatiana: you remember albania because you think
of me, yes?

chessman: well, not really

Tatiana: you not think of me??

chessman: no. i mean yes. of course i think
of you. but...

Tatiana: there. i knew it. i have instincts of
this thinking

chessman: what do you mean?

Tatiana: instincts? is not correct?

chessman: i'm not sure. like a preposition?
i mean premonition? like a dream?
an intuition?

Tatiana: an intuition, let me say. i will tell it you
like this.

late in the night, i am look to the stars over my beautiful sad country of albania, and i am thinking yes, somewhere, somewhere in atlanta usa is brilliant and handsome young man who is think of me this very minute

chessman: that's... um, well, that's very nice of you to tell me

Tatiana: a sweet man on whom these same stars will shine tonight

chessman: um...

Tatiana: and this man is you, i am so sure

chessman: you are?

Tatiana: in my heart, i know this

chessman: you do?

Tatiana: an intuition. so for you to say of course you think of me—oh, mitchell, i have not the words in english to say it, how beautiful this to me is

chessman: well... um

Tatiana: this is fine for me to tell you?

chessman: i think so. but...

Tatiana: not too much of the passion?

chessman: um, tatiana, i should explain something

Tatiana: of course. please to explain me. i listen to all that you say with my open heart

Bridget has entered

Bridget: hello, good morning

Tatiana: bridget! hallo my english friend

Big.J has entered

Big.J: johnson's here, ladies and germs. what up what up?

Tatiana: johnson, you are the late one, i think. 15 minute

Bridget: hello, mr. johnson

Big.J: is it that late already?

chessman: johnson, listen. beau's here in a minute, and i really gotta bounce

Tatiana: you really bounce?

Bridget: lol. i think he means he needs 2 leave early

chessman: um, right. sorry. leave early. gotta go

Big.J: whoa whoa. hold on there. young feller

Iatiana: wait mitchell. you were to explain me something, i did think?

Big.J: yes, leave us not in contumelious haste

Bridget: contumelious?

BoBoy has entered

BoBoy: word up, dawgs, sorry i'm late

chessman: dude. there you are. hey, sorry gotta go

BoBoy: i beg yr stuff?

Big.J: mitchie's trying 2 bail on us

chessman: yeah, remember? i have that thing

Tatiana: a thing?

BoBoy: **what thing, dude?**

chessman: see you later all

Tatiana: but i thought you were to explain

chessman has left the room

Tatiana: ah, there he goes

BoBoy: **weird. he doesn't have a thing. it's the middle of the nite**

Big.J: he's escaping. what did u say 2 him Tatiana?

Bridget: oh, that IS 2 bad. how very tiresome.

Big.J: what was he going 2 explain?

Tatiana: he didn't say

BoBoy: **how dreary**

Tatiana: he only say he must explain to me something, and i say i am listening to hear what it is

Bridget: really? i didn't catch any of that

Tatiana: it was only before you entered the chatting room

Bridget: oic

Tatiana: i will have to, um, ask it out of him in another day

Big.J: zackly. slap him around l8r. there's plenty of time

Tatiana: slap him? that would be difficult

Big.J: a figure of speech

Tatiana: how strange a thing of you to say

BoBoy: **lol. mitch might just like a little spanking now and then**

Bridget: beg pardon? whatever do u mean?

Big.J: well, a man does like a woman 2 show some fire

Bridget: really

Tatiana: in my country, i was telling mitchell, women are full of the passion. is unusual for america?

Bridget: yes, is it unusual?

Big.J: um no, not unusual. not at all

Bridget: 4 example, i'm sure mitch has a very passionate girlfriend

Tatiana: he has girlfriend? he say nothing of her to me

Big.J: u'd have 2 ask him how passionate she is. let's just say that some american women r a little reserved

Bridget: is that a fact?

BoBoy: **not my girl, dude**

Tatiana: no? your girl is passionate one?

Big.J: tamra's a fine person. very fine

BoBoy: **passion like a racehorse. like a steamroller**

Tatiana: excuse? your girl is a horse? and she rollers over you?

Big.J: dude, <cough cough> if she heard u say that, she'd dope-slap u into next week

Tatiana: she slaps, too? you don't say

Big.J: no no no. just kidding around.
              ms. T is a peach of a girl

BoBoy: **lol. she's a peach all right. yum**

Tatiana: i am so confused. she is this horse first,
              then a road equipment, now a food. if you
              not like this girl, why you would keep her?

Bridget: tatiana, did mitch say his girl isn't passionate?

Tatiana: no no, my friend, he said nothing of
              complaint about his girl to me. unlike
              Mr. BoBoy here

Bridget: u must know her, beau?

BoBoy: **bliss is a peach too**

Tatiana: a peach

BoBoy: **mitchie don't complain, i guarantee**

Big.J: yes, a real peach, that girl.
              what a sweetie

Tatiana: sorry, sorry. excuse me very much.
              but peach is fruit, correct?

Bridget: yes, that's right

Tatiana: so. the girl is something to chew up?
              and then—how do you say?—to spit
              away the center

Big.J: oh please. it's just a figure
              of speech

BoBoy: **yeah**

Tatiana: meaning?

Big.J: ok. meaning, um, creative,
              generous, kind, yet... full
              of character

Tatiana: hmm

BoBoy: and delicious ;-)

Tatiana: excuse me?

Big.J: he means delicious to the spirit!
            to the heart

BoBoy: what?

Tatiana: is how you see a woman this way, beau?
            a fruit to be sliced and swallowed and spit
            away? how extraordinary

Big.J: really, tatiana. it's not
            offensive. it's a southern
            thing. hard 2 explain

BoBoy: yeah, southern

Big.J: yeah

Tatiana: and other times a horse beast for racing and
            breeding, and other times a truck machine
            for flattening the road?

BoBoy: u make it almost like degratory

Tatiana: ah. now you begin to see.

Big.J: please please, tatiana, all this
            about peach? peachy? peach-i-tude?

Tatiana: i cannot say it's something i would like to be
            called

**BoBoy: dude, my grandmother says it all the time, and
            she doesn't have a degratory bone in her body**

Big.J: not a bone

BoBoy: yeah

Tatiana: hmm, and sometimes to you i am even dude,
            which is, i think, a casual BOY acquaintance?

Big.J: bro, u just painted us into a corner

BoBoy: what i say? what i say?

Tatiana: excuse me so much, but, talking of
            grandmothers, mine is on the next room calling
            to me. i must say goodbye for today

Tatiana has left the room

Bridget: oh, she's gone away mad. how dreadful

Big.J: that was weird

BoBoy: we ticked her off, didn't we?

Bridget: u think????

BoBoy: now i feel bad

Big.J: aw man. she can't really be
            offended by "peach" can she?
            how lame is that?

Bridget: i thought u liked yr women passionate

Big.J: i like em reasonable too. jeeze

Bridget: she's lame because u offended her?

Big.J: no, because she's a femi-nazi

BoBoy: it didn't offend u, did it?

Bridget: maybe i'm not passionate enuf

BoBoy: i can't believe that

Bridget: she's smarter than me. that counts

Big.J: whatever. uh, listen, bro. britt
            just popped up. can u hold down
            the fort 4 a while?

Bridget: another passionate woman, mr. johnson?

BoBoy: lol. u just got dissed in england, J

Big.J has left the room

Bridget: can i just say yr friend johnson is a difficult person
              2 like?

BoBoy: **really?**

Bridget: really

BoBoy: **aw, he's all right. a little sketchy, but he's cool.
              that's what mitch says**

Bridget: i get this feeling when i talk 2 him

BoBoy: **what feeling?**

Bridget: like my teeth r grinding and something is twisting in
              my stomach

BoBoy: **hey that's serious**

Bridget: i know i shouldn't feel that way

BoBoy: **no, that's ok. johnson can be hard 2 take**

Bridget: like he's not lying, but he twists words. like a politician

BoBoy: **ha'e a poet**

Bridget: whatever

BoBoy: **hey no problem. how u feel is how u feel**

Bridget: i don't know...

BoBoy: **u won't offend me, that's 4 sure**

Bridget: well, i'm glad of that

BoBoy: **totally**

Bridget: thanks

BoBoy: **take some deep breaths now. that always
              helps me**

Bridget: helps u? u get this way sometimes too?

BoBoy: sure. well, i mean, usually i'm a tank, a rock. but sometimes...

Bridget: sometimes u get steamrolled?

BoBoy: i shouldn't have said that, huh?

Bridget: no it's ok. she'll get over it

BoBoy: it's just, well, it seems like my girl is way ahead of me half the time

Bridget: yeah

BoBoy: like, i dunno. well, i'm not what u'd totally call smart and handsome

Bridget: oh please. i happen 2 know u r

BoBoy: dude! don't make fun of me

Bridget: i'm not

BoBoy: here i am getting all girly...

Bridget: i'm not!

BoBoy: whatever

Bridget: no i mean it, k? i just know ur plenty smart and really handsome

BoBoy: lol

Bridget: seriously. i can tell these things

BoBoy: well anyway...

Bridget: yeah?

BoBoy: i just mean... k, i'm not complaining about ms. T, but sometimes i just feel like she's too smart 4 me

Bridget: i know. i totally feel that way

BoBoy: she really is—and gorgeous too. and, well i get these feelings like... i dunno. like she might find someone else

Bridget: absolutely. me too

BoBoy: **but really i'm like in awe of her**

Bridget: right. i have the same fear about my... chap

BoBoy: **seriously?**

Bridget: sure. he's totally beyond me sometimes, and i just get
             desperate when i think someone else might snatch him away.
             u know

BoBoy: **yes, i do know**

Bridget: so what do i do?

BoBoy: **no worries. there's nothing 2 do. just keep being yrself**

Bridget: that's it?

BoBoy: **sure! keep growing, keep loving him. he's with u
             4 a reason**

Bridget: i guess

BoBoy: **i learned that from my man mitch**

Bridget: mitch said that?

BoBoy: **when i worry about T, he says, dude, she chose u,
             and she wouldn't hook up with a bonehead**

Bridget: that's a nice thing 2 say

BoBoy: **yeah**

Bridget: u really like this girl, don't u?

BoBoy: **she's a real... oh, oops, i'm not going 2 say that again**

Bridget: lol

BoBoy: **ha**

Bridget: ur a funny guy. i never knew that... about americans, i mean

BoBoy: **oh sure. keep em laughing, that's what i always say**

Bridget: it's so easy 2 talk 2 u

BoBoy: **well...**

Bridget: how i feel is... what did u say?

BoBoy: **it's how u feel. can't blame yrself 4 that**

Bridget: ur nice. ur a nice boy, beau... beau boy.

BoBoy: **:)**

Bridget: well...

BoBoy: **what u thinkin?**

Bridget: dunno... i shouldn't say

BoBoy: **come on. i won't tell**

Bridget: it's just... listen, um...

BoBoy: **i'm listenin**

Bridget: ok, what if i felt... oh i don't know

BoBoy: **what?**

Bridget: oh, i'm too comfortable with u. it's like i could tell u anything. anything at all

BoBoy: **u CAN tell me anything, bridget. of course u can**

Bridget: i really shouldn't

BoBoy: **no, what? seriously**

Bridget: well, like what if i felt something 4 u?

BoBoy: **wow. really?**

Bridget: i mean, nothing that would get u in trouble. but...

BoBoy: **but what?**

Bridget: well. put it this way. if a certain american chap was ever free to look around...

BoBoy: yes?

Bridget: then he wouldn't have 2 look far

BoBoy: sweet. just over in england?

Bridget: maybe england's not that far :) but seriously, is that ok?

BoBoy: bridge, honey, that is just the nicest thing 2 say

Bridget: so ur ok with it?

BoBoy: well, it's like u say, IF a person was available

Bridget: yeah

BoBoy: which i'm not, technically

Bridget: technically?

BoBoy: well, T is gone all summer it looks like

Bridget: oic

BoBoy: but can i tell u something?

Bridget: what?

BoBoy: if i really was a single dude, i'd be looking at england in a heartbeat

Bridget: awww, u know what, beau boy?

BoBoy: what?

Bridget: ur a peach

CHAPTER 10
grounded

THE DAWG HOUSE

JUNE 08 07:30 PM

Big.J has entered

BoBoy: j-man, sup?

Big.J: mitch boy, u bailed on me.
that ain't right

chessman: i had to. sorry

Big.J: HAD 2? what's HAD 2?

chessman: it is what it is. get over it

Big.J: dude, i gotta tell u this is
totally TOTALLY against the code

chessman: what? there's no code

BoBoy: yeah, mitch. the code of the south

Big.J: never give up. never surrender

chessman: get outta town

Big.J: may the farce be with u

chessman: i didn't give up. i made a decision

Big.J: decision 2 give up, u mean

BoBoy: so, mitch. ur out?

chessman: looks like it, bro

BoBoy: dude, i thought u were the stable 1

chessman: yeah, well

Big.J: u can't bail, mitch

chessman: watch me

BoBoy: but why? what happened?

Big.J: we had a deal

BoBoy: no really, what happened? i show up, and ur
            gone right now

chessman: i don't know. i was just getting
            a feeling

Big.J: wait a minute...

BoBoy: u got the BRAINS, dude. I'M sposed to get the
            feelings. this isn't fair

Big.J: wait a minute. he and tatiana
            were there b4 us

BoBoy: as in alone?

Big.J: what i'm sayin

chessman: not my idea

Big.J: bro, she hit on u, didn't she?

BoBoy: tanny from alBANNy? hit on ol mitch?

Big.J: that's what i'm thinkin

chessman: albania

BoBoy: u dawg u!

chessman: hey, i did nothing!

BoBoy: u stinkin dawg. way 2 go!

Big.J: that's it, isn't it, mitchie?

chessman: maybe

BoBoy: what a hound

Big.J: k listen, dude, that's no reason
2 bail

BoBoy: what did she say?

chessman: she was just, i dunno. she said
some stuff

Big.J: gimme a break

BoBoy: like what? what did she say, bro?

chessman: nah, man, i'm not going there

Big.J: whatta wuss

BoBoy: come on, mitch boy, u gotta give us something

Big.J: seriously, how bad could it be?

chessman: i'm honestly not sure. but bad
enough

Big.J: but i mean she's in freakin italy
or somewhere

chessman: ALBANIA. would someone tell me why
it's SO hard to remember ALBANIA?

BoBoy: ...oh he likes her

Big.J: oh man

BoBoy: k, now u really gotta tell us what she said

chessman: talk to the hand

Big.J: no, that's cool, bro. we can
            fill in this part ourselves

BoBoy: yeah, we know what she said. let's see... johnson?

Big.J: no, i got it. she talked about...
            oh, dude. passion, right?

chessman: maybe

Big.J: k, stop me if u've heard this 1.
            ahem: ALBANIAN women r passionate.
            they're VERY passionate. they
            basically have passion in the water

BoBoy: nice

Big.J: and she's in fact been having
            some thoughts lately about mitchell
            back in (how does she say it?) back
            in atlanta usa

BoBoy: no way. is he right, bro?

chessman: he isn't wrong

BoBoy: oh u dawg

Big.J: first she gets misty <sigh>,
            then she comes on like a little
            strong 4 u. she says, hmm,
            something about... stars

chessman: bite me

BoBoy: amazing, J. how do u do it? <fist bump>

Big.J: it's the poetry. nothing 2 it

BoBoy: mitch boy, did u even tell her about bliss??

chessman: i tried... honest i did

BoBoy: **dude, ur toast**

chessman: she wouldn't listen

Big.J: course not. she's a poet. no...
no, that girl is poetry itself

chessman: it was like holding off a team
of girl cousins

BoBoy: **lol**

chessman: i'm like, dude, i need to tell
you something, but she's all
mitchell, mitchell you're so sweet
to think of me. you DO think of me,
don't you mitchell?

BoBoy: **oh man**

chessman: and i go, um, i wasn't really
thinking of you that way, ok? and
she's like what?? you never think
of me?? i break-a you fingers. and
i go, no no, i DO think of you,
just not like THAT, only she doesn't
hear the "not like that" part

BoBoy: **oh man**

chessman: then she's all, oh mitchell, i
knew it, and then, THEN, she
goes totally over the top. oh at
night I am look at the stars over
my beautiful passionate freakin
homeland, and I am think of you
thinking of me thinking of you, and
i pray for the stars to be shining
on you in usa... and i'm like, oh
please, this canNOT be happening

BoBoy: **oh man oh man oh man**

Big.J: did i nail it, bo boy?

BoBoy: u da man, J

Big.J: oh, wait, so that was what
she meant about he was going
2 explain something

chessman: i guess. did she say that?

BoBoy: oh yeah. she kept on that 4 a while

Big.J: until bubba pissed her off

BoBoy: hey

chessman: you did? what did you say?

BoBoy: not me! it was johnson

Big.J: u wish, dude. i wasn't the 1
objectifying all the women in
the room

chessman: aw man

BoBoy: objectionizing? i don't know nuffin bout this,
mitch, i swear

chessman: come on, what happened?

Big.J: funny how i remember it so
differently...

BoBoy: mitch, she's wild. u know what i'm talkin about.
when she gets her teeth into u, she's totally a steam—

oops

Big.J: a steamroller. see, mitch?

chessman: man, you can't say stuff like that

Big.J: zackly. a steamroller with
teeth? mixed metaphors r totally
out of line

chessman: no dude, you can't call a woman
things that are... well, THINGS

Big.J: oh that. right

BoBoy: i know i know i know. i know NOW. tatiana
            totally went cold on us

chessman: man

Big.J: she had the nerve 2 cross-examine
            me. ME of all people

chessman: about what?

Big.J: totally uncalled 4

BoBoy: left the room in a snit

chessman: about what?

BoBoy: just don't call her a peach, that's all i can say

chessman: well, duh

BoBoy: come on. my granny says that all the time.
            now he was a nice man—a real peach. do u
            hear dudes complaining? i don't think so

chessman: but it's different with guys

Big.J: the english chick didn't seem
            2 mind

BoBoy: yeah. i was talkin 2 her later

chessman: man, i hope you didn't say chick
            to her

BoBoy: well, u know what i mean

chessman: how long did you talk to her?

BoBoy: i dunno. awhile after johnson left

chessman: you tell her about tamra?

BoBoy: um?

Big.J: ooo la la, i knew it

BoBoy: no i did. i think i did

Big.J: of course he didn't

chessman: aw, beau... what were you thinking?

Big.J: oh u people need 2 get over
           yrselves

chessman: easy for you to say, poetry man

BoBoy: **skanks aplenty, skanks galore**

Big.J: i mean. why WOULD he tell her
           about T?

BoBoy: **um, wait. i think i know this one**

chessman: because ms. T isn't brittney.
           show some respect

BoBoy: **thanks, man**

Big.J: brittney? easy there, cowboy

chessman: or what, skank boy?

Big.J: chill, mitchie. brittney is
           very fragile right now

chessman: we know. she's needy, you keep
           saying

BoBoy: **wait. she's fragile?**

Big.J: fragile i said, and fragile it is

BoBoy: **dude, what have u done?**

Big.J: let's just say i won't have u
           dissin my ex-girlfriends

chessman: oh man

BoBoy: **i knew it. i knew it**

Big.J: chill out, boyz. she'll be fine

BoBoy: **what is that—like 9 days?? bro, yr license 2
           love is hereby revocated**

```
chessman:   totally. you're grounded, J

Big.J:      get out

chessman:   no, you are

BoBoy:      it's outta control

chessman:   you get no more cooperation from
            us until you straighten out ·

Big.J:      slow down, dudes. as much as we
            appreciate yr concern 4 the J man,
            we must say ur crossing a
            line here

chessman:   dude, say nothing. you've lost
            all credibility

BoBoy:      and now ur startin 2 reflect on yr bros

Big.J:      well mercy me. we're worried
            about our reputation, r we?

chessman:   we're worried about YOU, man

BoBoy:      dude, ur a train wreck on wheels

chessman:   you can't use people up and toss
            them aside like... i don't know

BoBoy:      like peach pits

Big.J:      lol

chessman:   seriously, J. you don't want to
            do people that way

Big.J:      aw man, he's gone 2 church on
            me now

chessman:   you don't want to be carrying
            all those broken hearts

Big.J:      i always lay them down gently,
            thank u ;-)
```

BoBoy: nah. u carry them. i can c it, dude

chessman: you don't have to agree with us, J

Big.J: thank u

chessman: but here's the thing. we're out
of the chat room unless you grow up

Big.J: is that so?

BoBoy: u got it

chessman: he needs to... what, beau? totally
stay away from women?

BoBoy: except in the chat room

chessman: where we can supervise you

BoBoy: that's it

Big.J: sure... that could happen

chessman: and with them, you have to pay
attention, you have to show some
class, and... let's see...

Big.J: u done yet, mother mitchell?

BoBoy: u have 2 make em like u

chessman: those are the terms, johnson. make
em like you

Big.J: ur such little girls

BoBoy: J, ur messin up their life and yr life too

Big.J: it's MY life. if i want 2 mess
it up i will

BoBoy: no, that won't work, bro. sorry

chessman: we know you don't like criticism,
so take it as a challenge

BoBoy: sure! it's just retraining the mind. u have a strong mind

Big.J: and u people have me confused with someone who cares

chessman: come ON, johnson. for your own good. you know it's a problem

BoBoy: even annie said it's a problem

Big.J: no she didn't

BoBoy: she totally did

chessman: well, annie's hard core, beau. can anyone please her?

BoBoy: he's afraid he can't do it. especially with annie...

chessman: he's too used to skanks

Big.J: k. u can just chill with that, mitch

BoBoy: it's a poet's challenge, J. c what u can do

Big.J: that is so lame

chessman: seriously, bro. bottom line is we're outta here unless you buy in

Big.J: whatever

chessman: ok sure. you'll hardly miss us

BoBoy: just makes yr summer school a little tougher. that's all

Big.J: @#$%!*

BoBoy: really J. friends don't let friends self-destruct

Big.J: ur SO over the line with this

BoBoy: oh nooooo! we crossed the line...

chessman: so move the line, J. i know you can
see SOME way this will work for you

BoBoy: or not. either way is cool with us

Big.J: don't bluff me

chessman: nobody's bluffing, bro. WE don't
have summer school

Big.J: okokok

BoBoy: aight then

Big.J: just hold up a minute

chessman: ok, here's where he tries his
own bluff...

Big.J: look. it's true that i still
need u bozos 2 finish the chat room

BoBoy: there u go, J boy

Big.J: that's the only reason i would
do this yr way

BoBoy: c... he needs us

chessman: i can live with that

Big.J: plus, well... honestly... i've
<ahem> got my eye on a very
interesting number lately who may
require a different approach

BoBoy: aw johnson...

chessman: no, that's ok. different approach
is good. but not till after the chat
room is over, got it?

Big.J: whatever. fine

BoBoy: fine

chessman: fine

Big.J: but here's MY condition

chessman: he's incorrigible

BoBoy: **he's what? that's not good, is it?**

Big.J: the condition is that NOBODY
bails until this is over. got
it girls? no mitchie running away.
no bubba getting cold feet. for
2 more weeks, i belong 2 summer
school, and u punks belong 2 me.

chessman: <sigh> fair enough, bo?

BoBoy: **i'm there**

Big.J: after that, skanks of the
world unite. Big.J is back in
circulation!

CHAPTER 11
politics

GURLGANG ROOM
JUNE 08 08:30 PM

gothling: now THAT was good work last night, ladies. i read johnson's transcript. very very nice.

bliss4u: did u think so?

gothling: i thought u were especially good with beau this time

bliss4u: really?

gothling: awesome. nice back and forth. u stayed a step ahead, then u left him with a sweet little wink

Ms.T: really? what was that? i left early

bliss4u: oh, i said he was a peach

Ms.T: you didn't!

bliss4u: well, bridget did. and besides it was true

gothling: **it was excellent. true or not, it worked**

Ms.T: worked? i spent like 50 lines telling them not to say that stuff

gothling: **exactly why bliss should say it**

bliss4u: i just thought it would make him feel better

gothling: **right. u soothed the male ego**

Ms.T: stab me in the back, why don't you?

bliss4u: why?? what's wrong with calling him a peach?

Ms.T: what's wrong is i don't want him saying stuff like that. duh...

gothling: **tam, ur outta line. bridget isn't yr lil yes-gurl. besides, he didn't know he was talking 2 u when he had that convo**

Ms.T: that doesn't matter

gothling: **it matters because he doesn't take his housetraining from tatiana — only from tamra**

bliss4u: housetraining? that's cold, annie

gothling: **oh, he does whatever T says. and hey, i was giving u props, girl. don't u come after me now**

bliss4u: i'm just saying

Ms.T: he needs to see that women agree on this

gothling: **well, tam, women DON'T agree on it. so he learns 2 read the signs**

Big.J has entered

Big.J: allo allo?

gothling: **johnson, what up? nice of u 2 break in**

Big.J: word. hey i just wanted 2 say how well lady bridget, lady tatiana did last night. well done well done

Ms.T: johnson, frankly, i'm not feeling approachable right now. so before you compliment me, do me a favor?

Big.J: at yr service, miss

Ms.T: change your username

bliss4u: lol, tam. gotta agree with u on this one

Big.J: beg pardon?

gothlIng: **oh 4... johnson, u really caught her in a mood this time. sorry**

Ms.T: i am not in a mood, annie. i've always hated his username. it's offensive

Big.J: yeah, but i really don't get it. my username? ah. oh, NOW i c. heh heh. never thought of that. hmm. well, k. give me a moment

Big.J has left the room

gothlIng: **tam, this is uncalled for, don't u think?**

Ms.T: oh, like he should get to be crude to us, just because he's your friend?

gothling: **no. but he shouldn't have 2 toe any line u just happen 2 draw**

bliss4u: i'm with tam. it's an offense 2 all womankind

gothling: **u chicks r totally putting me off. i thought we were going 2 have a nice evening of bonding and affirming. gurl stuff**

Mr.Jeeves has entered

Mr.Jeeves: better?

gothling: **oh, johnson, i don't know...**

bliss4u: lol. much better

Ms.T: puts a whole different leer on your face

gothling: i just don't like it, J

Mr.Jeeves: really? what's wrong with it?

gothling: well, in a nutshell, ur not their butler

Mr.Jeeves: ah. true... is that important?

Ms.T: but he could stand to play the role for a while :)

gothling: i don't think so

bliss4u: now who's being picky?

gothling: ur nobody's servant, johnson. be a man

Ms.T: leave it, johnson. we like it

gothling: absolutely not

Mr.Jeeves: not a problem, annie dear. be right back

Mr.Jeeves has left the room

bliss4u: u guys r kinda pushing him around

Ms.T: yeah. the irony of this is lost on no one,
                  annie

bliss4u: what irony?

Ms.T: "ur nobody's servant. now go change yr
                  name"

gothling: at least i don't force my politics on people

Ms.T: you just did! everything is politics, annie.
                  you know that

bliss4u: not 2 me. somewhere u stop and
                  it's just people

Ms.T: people are never just people

bliss4u: ur SO twitchy 2nite, girl

gothling: **she's mad because she can't control beau when he's outta sight.**

Ms.T: i'm FINE. lay off

gothling: **grow up. this all started when u found out that bliss and beau r getting along**

bliss4u: hey, i didn't do anything. i just said he was a peach

gothling: **which he is...**

Ms.T: oh, shut up, you two. i wanna know why johnson is being so... whatever he's being

gothling: **he's being friendly. maybe u've heard of that?**

bliss4u: lol annie

Ms.T: he's being TOO friendly

bliss4u: well, u did say u wouldn't talk 2 him if he didn't change his name

Ms.T: his name was crude. i just didn't expect him to give up without a fight

gothling: **listen, T. this has 2 stop. u can't just dictate 2 everyone**

Ms.T: i didn't think i was dictating. i thought we all wanted to get along

bliss4u: we do!

Ms.T: then we have to respect each other's point of view

gothling: **exactly! so show johnson some respect**

alfonso has entered

alfonso: so i'm don alfonso this time. from cosi fan tutte? like it?

Ms.T: fine with me

alfonso:	any objections 2 mozart? opera? the whole 18th century?
Ms.T:	it's a fine name, johnson
gothling:	**k, r we done?**
alfonso:	not too albanian 4 u?
bliss4u:	lol
alfonso:	oh look, i made bliss laugh. that goes on my calendar
gothling:	**johnson, we're kind of into a gurl fight here. can u make it quick?**
alfonso:	oic. well <cough cough> i just stopped by 2 say how well i thought u kids did last night. not kids. um, ladies?
gothling:	**that's it?**
alfonso:	well, they both had some inspired moments, didn't u think, annie?
gothling:	**that's where i STARTED this convo. but SOME people have CONTROL issues**
alfonso:	lol. but not miss annie, right? no control issues there...
Ms.T:	now that's the first amusing thing you've ever said, johnson. you may stay 2 extra minutes just for that
alfonso:	yow! that's both of them now. i made em both smile!
gothling:	**don't push it, J**
alfonso:	btw, T. i looked back at the transcript on u and mitch. why do u think he freaked?
Ms.T:	duh. i scared him off. i misjudged his devotion to our bliss girl

bliss4u: \<sigh\>

alfonso: i was surprised too. i didn't think u were that aggressive... i thought he would be flattered

Ms.T: you never know

gothling: no, johnson's right. he should have been flattered, and i think he was

bliss4u: huh?

gothling: that's what scared him. tatiana got 2 him

Ms.T: you think? actually, i was rather.hurt when he disappeared

alfonso: annie makes total sense. tatiana got 2 him

bliss4u: hey, wait a sec. how about he just didn't want 2 cheat on me?

alfonso: well, yes. the simplest answer. and what he said later fits with that

bliss4u: there, u see?

alfonso: still, he may ALSO have been embarrassed... by how he felt. i've been chatting with the boyz, and i do see a glimmer of something there

bliss4u: oh please

alfonso: tatiana's a fascinating gurl. credit where it's due

Ms.T: thank you

bliss4u: but he didn't DO anything

alfonso: quite true. so it's win-win 4 bliss and tam

Ms.T: but another loss for annie

gothling: i can wait. he's on the hook

alfonso: they both r. beau boy was tongue-tied after talking with bridget

Ms.T:	yeah, with miss peach
alfonso:	actually, interesting thing, T. did u know the only 1 who gets u on politics is mitch?
bliss4u:	why? what did he say?
alfonso:	he totally reamed beau and me
Ms.T:	really?
alfonso:	i kid u not. we explained about calling u a peach, and he was all "dude, u can't call a chick things."
	(not chick. a woman. my bad. mitch never says chick)
bliss4u:	why can't u call a chick things?
Ms.T:	bliss, puhleeeze...
bliss4u:	whatever. it's a word
alfonso:	u can't call them... like, a thing, i guess. an object
bliss4u:	but...
alfonso:	i know i know. but what i mean is mitch gets this stuff. he GETS it. and honestly? it's really starting 2 change my way of seeing things
gothling:	**u don't say**
bliss4u:	i just don't c what there is 2 get
Ms.T:	bliss, come on. has mitch ever called you an animal or a thing, or something associated with children?
bliss4u:	i don't think so. just nice things, like he says i'm pretty or my hair is cute or something
Ms.T:	i rest my case
gothling:	**why?? that proves nothing**

Ms.T: it proves he respects her, duh. i'm not saying that, like, peach and ho are equal, ok? but they both make her less than human. THAT's what mitch gets

gothling: **unlike beau?**

alfonso: annie, let's don't go all tense, please

gothling: **unlike beau, tamra??**

Ms.T: ok, annie. yes. unlike beau

gothling: **now we're gettin 2 it**

Ms.T: beau doesn't have a clue, ok annie? beau speaks of me like an object sometimes, ok? beau doesn't respect me the way mitch respects bliss

bliss4u: tamra, ur up in the nite! beau totally luvs u

Ms.T: right. that's why he hit on you

bliss4u: but he didn't...

Ms.T: and he hit on you because you don't CONTROL him. because whatever he says is just so damn cute to you. it's just a word with no meaning, no history, no politics. you just jiggle your pompoms and nod your empty head

alfonso: tamra, if i may interject a word here...

Ms.T: how would you know if beau respects you or not, bliss? you don't have any more of a clue than he does

bliss4u: shut up, T. just shut up right now

Ms.T: actually, you're perfect for each other. two freakin clueless blind chauvinistic middle-brow morons. i hope you're happy together, because i'm outta here

Ms.T is offline

gothling: **oooo la LA**

alfonso: well, i was afraid of this

bliss4u: i am SO not speaking 2 her

CHAPTER 12
a new leaf

✉ IM from gothling

gothling: yo johnson

alfonso: si si, dorabella?

gothling: dorabella? k, dude. what r u listening 2 right now?

alfonso: um, nothing. nothing at all

gothling: spit it out. something euro. something classical

alfonso: no way. u know me. i only do edgy stuff: gnarls, belle & sebastian. white stripes. um?

gothling: nice try

alfonso: bob marley? classic tupac? the supremes?

gothling: it's opera isn't it?

alfonso: okok, it's mozart! i won't apologize

gothling: busted

alfonso: get out. mozart is my only solace. he brings order 2 chaos and darkness

gothling: <yawn>

alfonso: annie, dear, tell me u feel it too. the encroaching gloom

gothling: oh, that's yr senior year coming, pal. push through the curtain and the light will dawn

alfonso: yes, like sunrise at the landfill. that's what i'm afraid of. i'm waking just in time 2 see where my life is ending

gothling: get a grip

alfonso: u could take me seriously... 4 once

gothling: earn it, scooter

alfonso: oh annie, if that were possible. ur a forbidding and formidable woman. how would anyone earn yr regard?

gothling: such a wit, johnson...

alfonso: if only u meant that

gothling: which reminds me. how come u never wrote me a poem?

alfonso: huh? maybe because u despise me?

gothling: oh, i do not. u write them 4 class, 4 the yearbook. 4 every girl u know. everyone thinks it's so random, but they're all totally in awe

alfonso: true, true

gothling: and ur, like, dr. bartolo's favorite student

alfonso: jeeze, gurl. don't ruin it

gothling: so why no poem 4 me?

alfonso: annabelle

gothling: what am i... a potted plant?

alfonso: sweetie...

gothling: what?

alfonso: i am totally certain this is not why u IM'd me

gothling: true. but it's still a good question. i think it just shows how u been neglecting me all these years <sigh>

alfonso: k, now ur scaring me. how bout this: u tell me why ur really here, and i promise 2 write a poem just 2 make u stop this line of talk

gothling: easy. i'm here, my child, because i want 2 know what ur up 2

alfonso: ah

gothling: so? what's with the nicey niceness 2 tam and bliss all of a sudden?

alfonso: well, not unexpected... how shall i?... let's say i'm turning over a new leaf

gothling: a new leaf

alfonso: mmm. temporarily at least

gothling: temporarily

alfonso: until this chat room stuff is over and bartolo signs off on my genius once again <sigh>

gothling: dude, what's this about? do i need 2 come by and pound some sense into u?

alfonso: tempting—and thanks—but no. this is something i have 2 do. and i'm actually quite reconciled 2 it

gothling: i'm waiting

alfonso: well, it truly does have 2 do with saving our little chat room. mitch and beau have laid down the law. it's absurd.... yet the absurdity does give it a certain appeal

gothling: stop blathering and talk 2 me

alfonso: ok, try this: either i mend my ways or the dudes drop out of the chat room

gothling: that's blackmail!

alfonso: u got it

gothling: totally out of line. what is their problem?

alfonso: they, um, heard about brittney

gothling: what about her?

alfonso: they feel i was perhaps not entirely... fair 2 her

gothling: oh, like u should have married her

alfonso: well. i believe mitch and beau see her as part of a pattern

gothling: of course there's a pattern. hello?? ur a total screwup with women. why they love u i don't know

alfonso: it's a gift

gothling: i'm gonna dope slap u, boy. u don't respect women. u think u love them, but u don't. u collect em and discard em. ur a cliché

alfonso: let it out, annie.... don't hold back just out of politeness...

gothling: oh, get a grip. i'm not mad, johnson. i'm not tamra. besides, it's fun 2 watch

alfonso: thank u so much

gothling: but ur a classic southern male. selfish, thoughtless, pretentious, and dumber than soap

alfonso: pretentious? moi?

gothling: AND afraid of commitment

alfonso: now, that one's a wee bit true

gothling: well, duh, bubba. that's why u go 4 skanks. brittney and tiffany were only the last 2

alfonso: true, there were 1 or 2 others

gothling: lol. let's see... meg was yr little easter bunny. beth was in yr xmas stocking

alfonso: i'm so flattered that u noticed

gothling: and b4 her, it was anne-ellen, frankie... i'm missing 1...

alfonso: kami... michele... that's it, i think, 4 this school year

gothling: dawg, u do need a rest. u just ate through the whole buffet at hooters

alfonso: so now ur on their side?

gothling: of course not, doll. they may be right, but they're totally wrong

alfonso: say again?

gothling: just because there's a problem doesn't mean it's fixable

alfonso: excellent. ur really cheering me up

gothling: hey, u drove here all by yrself. i'm just blowing the horn

alfonso: u totally have no respect 4 me, do u?

gothling: of course i do, honey. i just don't expect u 2 act against yr nature

alfonso: how do u mean that?

gothling: ur a slut puppy. why fight it?

alfonso: luv u too

gothling: oh get over it

alfonso: monster. dragon lady

gothling: worm. insect

alfonso: asp

gothling: what? asp?

alfonso: a venomous snake, duh

gothling: kewl

alfonso: only bites u in the heart. ask cleopatra

gothling: aw, that's sweet. k, i gotta bounce. listen, don't let the blackmailers get u down. we're about to put them in their place

alfonso: hmm. that's true, i guess

gothling: totally. don't lose focus, babe. we finish this and then ur free again

alfonso: right. it's just that...

gothling: just what? there's no just anything

alfonso: just... well, remember when i made bliss laugh? she never gave me the time of day before. now i've made her laugh, and... i dunno...

gothling: johnson if u hit on her, i will personally mess u up

alfonso: ah. so u feel it could be a problem. what about tamra? i think i could be a totally new man with her

gothling: u try either 1, dude, and mitch and beau will have to stand in line. clear enough?

alfonso: i think i got it. still, it shows the potential

gothling: whatever. ok, bro. IM 2nite while they're in the chat room

gothling is off-line

alfonso: oh annie

annie annie annie

annie

In the Cards
10 JUNE

The cards do not lie, my friend.
—Ulrica the Witch, lame old gypsy saying

Joy and peace, camper. Today, back by popular demand: Uncle Jerry's Tarot Tent. Gloomy in here? Never you mind. Psychic truth is often found in shadows.

The cards do not lie, young camper, and why not? Because they do not care. How cold, you say, how dark. No, no, no. Think. Think how cold and dark your little world would be if the cards did care. Suppose they were to sugarcoat. Suppose they saw some danger lurking in your future and said nothing—just to spare your feelings. What a disaster. No, no, destiny must be faced with open eyes. If the cards cared, you could not trust them. And without trust, well, where would any of us be?

A quick three cards, my friend. The first... aww... two of cups. How dove-lovely. Two cups raised to lovers' lips. Two pairs of bright eyes meet.... But wait, this is in the past. *Tsk, tsk.* Oh please, don't weep, young camper. Lovers' lips may lie, but the cards do not.

Second card: eight of cups. Many things offer shiny promise, but today you find them cheap and empty. (We might say your cup runneth NOT over, heh heh heh. That's a joke, son. Psalm 23. Look it up; it'll do you good.) But how right you are. The world is full of false promise, and by the way, this is the subject of Uncle Jerry's latest online Sunday sermon, available now at a website near you. (You look like you could use a sermon, son, if I may say so.)

So, young camper, love is in the past, and the present does not satisfy. Ah me. Ah life. Let's move on. Card three: yes... the eight of wands. News approaching, the future unfolding. Tumult and shouting. But oh, how like the cards: The eight does not say *what* you will learn, my friend. It says only that knowledge will come, and *soon*.

So there it is. Destiny. For good or ill, it comes. Be brave. Beware. For as you know, the cards do not lie.

And neither does Your Uncle Jerry.

Joy and peace.

CHAPTER 13
friends

📧 IM from chessman

JUNE 10 04:00 PM

chessman: tatiana, are you there?

Tatiana: mitchell, how are you?

chessman: sorry to bother you. can you talk? i mean is now a good time?

Tatiana: you are never the bother, mitchell. is such a flattery that you would message over to me

chessman: thanks. i'm glad

Tatiana: one cannot say this of your friends

chessman: my friends. i was afraid of that. sorry

Tatiana: i regret only that i was not more rude to them

chessman: but that wouldn't be like you

Tatiana: i am no accustomed to be called so many unkind things

chessman: i'm sorry

Tatiana: horse, machine, boy, food

chessman: they called you a horse??

Tatiana: racehorse is kind of horse, correct?

chessman: yes, but surely they didn't mean you...

Tatiana: ah. they spoke of the girl who loves your friend. i take her side, for she was not there

chessman: oic

Tatiana: i am still furious about her, what they called

chessman: i'm not sure why you're angry about another girl

Tatiana: all women are one, mitchell

chessman: pardon?

Tatiana: no woman is fruit or steam engine. all are women. all are one

chessman: tatiana, maybe this was only a cross-cultural mistake? people must say things in albania that americans wouldn't really get. metaphors, like

Tatiana: racehorse is to say she is less than woman, correct? something driven by animal feelings?

chessman: but in albania...

Tatiana: if one say this in albania, you are talking of a not so very nice girl... and if one say it of me, my brothers will abuse one very badly about the head and shoulders. abuse is correct, yes?

chessman: tatiana, ok

ok, i apologize for my friends. they were ignorant and callous

Tatiana: they were pigs, dogs. hyenas

chessman: yes

Tatiana: and you apologize for them?

chessman: yes

Tatiana: you mean to defend them?

chessman: not at all. they were impolite to you. i apologize deeply

Tatiana: they were crude to all women everywhere

chessman: yes they were. i'm so sorry

Tatiana: and you have spoken to them about these words?

chessman: tatiana, i have abused them very badly

Tatiana: you have said a woman is not a horse?

chessman: i didn't know about the horse

Tatiana: then you must abuse them about the horse

chessman: yes, i will do that

Tatiana: no no, you must do it right now

chessman: ok. i'll go now and abuse them about the horse

Tatiana: and the dude

chessman: yes, the dude, too. they shouldn't say that

Tatiana: you tell them

chessman: yes. and tatiana?

Tatiana: what?

chessman: then may i talk to you later?

Tatiana: yes, perhaps i would like that

chessman: ok. goodbye for now

Tatiana: goodbye

chessman: see ya

Tatiana: mitchell?

chessman: yes?

Tatiana: you would never insult me, would you?

chessman: never. well, catch ya later

Tatiana: wait!

chessman: what?

Tatiana: where are you going? you cannot leave me now

chessman: but you said...

Tatiana: don't be silly. you can see i need your company

chessman: you do?

Tatiana: is obvious

chessman: ok, i'll stay then

Tatiana: oh, mitchell, just talking you make me feel so much better. talk me, talk me

chessman: um, ok. what shall i tell you?

Tatiana: anything about you. i must to know you so much better

chessman: well, i'm not very interesting

Tatiana: you ARE. you are so kind and so comforting. and there's much passion in you too. i feel as if you were going away to defend me just now.

chessman: well, i'm on your side...

Tatiana: is like the brother, or no—like the fiancé ;-)

chessman: well...

Tatiana: ah, so romantic :) mitchell and tatiana, ooo la la

chessman: um

Tatiana: i am flirting you, mitchell. do you see? like the fiancé...

chessman: yes, i thought you might be

Tatiana: hah. you are such the shy one. tell to me anything.

oh! you were to tell me something before. you have something to explain. you must tell me this

chessman: um, right now?

Tatiana: yes, of course right now. i demand it

chessman: well, in a way, it was about someone else

Tatiana: you must to tell me. i am all listening

chessman: this other person is a girl

Tatiana: hmph. a girl. she is a friend of you?

chessman: actually, she's my girlfriend. that's what i needed to tell you

Tatiana: your girlfriend

chessman: yes. i have a girlfriend

Tatiana: girlfriend is like the fiancée, yes?

chessman: yikes. no, we're too young for that. i really like her and stuff, but i've got college coming up and... you know

Tatiana: oic. the girlfriend is not the fiancée, but is still the special one

chessman: there you go. so...

Tatiana: so now there is problem?

chessman: so um, i don't know. but, well, maybe you shouldn't tell me about the stars and everything

Tatiana: because of this girl...

chessman: yeah

Tatiana: hmm. your girlfriend, she is passionate? possessive?

chessman: yes. well, maybe not like albanian women. but she and i don't see other people. we promised

Tatiana: so then no problem

chessman: really?

Tatiana: of course. you don't see me! on the internet, no one knows i am the dog. lol

chessman: nice one. but i'm sure you're not a dog, tatiana

Tatiana: you are too sweet for this girlfriend, i think, mitchell. she doesn't know how you are gallant and thoughtful

chessman: um? well, thanks... anyway, so it's ok to talk, but i don't think you should flirt with me. you know what i mean. you must have a boyfriend, right?

Tatiana: i fear not

chessman: i can't believe that. a passionate woman like you?

Tatiana: perhap i do have someone interested...

chessman: see there?

Tatiana: but i don't know how serious. i think i must work harder to make him more interested. is difficult, however

chessman: no way. what's the problem?

Tatiana: oh, he lives very far away

chessman: yeah, that's a tough one. my girlfriend has been out of town for weeks

Tatiana: he lives far away in america

chessman: in america?

Tatiana: but he likes me. i can sense it

chessman: you can?

Tatiana: oh yes. i must think how to win him away from his cold american girlfriend, lol

chessman: tatiana, please. you shouldn't flirt with me

Tatiana: sorry. sorry. i forget. don't be angry, mitchell

chessman: i'm not angry

Tatiana: i am harmless. don't be angry. just
teasing you

chessman: ok

Tatiana: i just like you. is this a crime?

chessman: no. but...

Tatiana: flirting is only how i show my liking. don't
worry, you are safe for your little american girlfriend

chessman: it makes me uncomfortable. i know it
shouldn't, but it does

Tatiana: ah, you worry so much about the girl. she's
gone, mitchell. she can't know what you say to me

chessman: that's really not the point

Tatiana: whatever, my darling. you are safe with tatiana

chessman: please don't

Tatiana: safe, safe, safe

chessman: ok but can we talk about something else?

Tatiana: yes! tell me something else: why does this girl
leave you?

chessman: she didn't leave me. she just went away for
a while

Tatiana: yes of course. but why did she?

chessman: her grandmother is ill

Tatiana: ah, poor grandmama

chessman: she had a stroke or something

Tatiana: you don't know?

chessman: well, she didn't know for sure when she left

Tatiana: but now?

chessman: i haven't heard from her

Tatiana: sorry? haven't heard from her about her dying grandmama and she is gone for months?

chessman: only a couple of weeks

Tatiana: well, she should be calling every day

chessman: it's complicated

Tatiana: twice every day. i would be calling you twice each day

chessman: no, it's cool

Tatiana: you don't miss her? good

chessman: sure i do. i just mean, if she can't call, then i understand

Tatiana: oh you trust her so much?

chessman: i do

Tatiana: what if she lies to you?

chessman: she doesn't. i know this girl. i know where she is

Tatiana: really. and where is that?

chessman: well, i don't know exactly. but i mean, i know that she's with her grandmother. and her friend tamra is with her too

Tatiana: hmph. this friend... what she is like?

chessman: oh, fantastic. i really like her

Tatiana: mitchell! so many girlfriends: me, the other, and now this tamra. you should be italian

chessman: lol. are you jealous?

Tatiana: fuming!

chessman: no seriously. tamra is famous around here. brains and beauty together. also very political. you'd like her

Tatiana: if she's after you, i despise her

chessman: not to worry. she's spoken for—my friend beau

Tatiana: racehorse woman? even so...

chessman: oh, you're so cynical. no, ms. T would never mess that up, certainly not with me

Tatiana: people do the strange thing, mitchell. but fine, let's put her to one side

chessman: tell me about your own life. got a boyfriend?

Tatiana: only the one in america

chessman: you're still flirting...

Tatiana: ah, ok. serious. i have almost 17 years old, i go to america for my year of school before university, and i have a boy—a boy name of... sebastien. sebastien max, whom i love too much

chessman: you love him too much? i didn't think that was possible for a passionate woman

Tatiana: now you are teasing me

chessman: see, you're brilliant, too

Tatiana: i am actually quite sad about this. i fear he falls in love with my friend

chessman: oh, no. really?

Tatiana: i am not sure, but is possible. i know she makes the play for him

chessman: tatiana, she doesn't have a chance

Tatiana: no, is possible. she is wonderful person, and i make many mistake

chessman: what do you mean by mistakes?

Tatiana: maybe i push too hard

chessman: on your boyfriend?

Tatiana: yes. i am so... i don't know how to say. like too much forceful sometime?

chessman: too intense?

Tatiana: si si. too intense many time. he is only a boy. he want more fun. i am more intense, more political like your girlfriend tamra

chessman: you're smarter than he is?

Tatiana: NO. everyone say this, but is not so. he is a fine mind. he is only more... social? he play, he laugh, he like the futbol

chessman: so he likes to take it easy, and you push yourself all the time

Tatiana: perhaps <sighing>

chessman: very hard to have a relationship like that. i'm so sorry

Tatiana: see how you understand everything? is too sad. mitchell, now you make me sad. why can you not love me just until i find another? your fiancée would never know

chessman: i'm sorry i make you sad. i could tell you a joke or something :-)

Tatiana: ha. that is a funny thing to say

chessman: ha. really i'm not a very funny guy. just ask my girlfriend

Tatiana: mitchell, here is the truth. the girlfriend sees only your surface, but you are deep water to me... i need you to be my friend. i am so alone sometime. always

chessman: i am your friend, tatiana

Tatiana: my friend and something perhaps more? a little?

chessman: tatiana, i'm sorry. i really can't

Tatiana: <sigh>

chessman: i know...

Tatiana: friends, then

chessman: friends

kissing lessons

📑 IM from Bridget

JUNE 10 08:00 PM

Bridget: beau? hello good evening?

BoBoy: bridge! hey girl, what up?

Bridget: surprised 2 hear from me?

BoBoy: sure am. what time is it over there?

Bridget: dunno. 5 hours later than u r

BoBoy: wow, 1 in the morning

Bridget: um i can't sleep 4 some reason

BoBoy: yeah, that happens 2 me

Bridget: tiresome

BoBoy: lol

Bridget: what?

BoBoy: tiresome. tired. can't sleep

Bridget: oic. sorry

BoBoy: just my sense of humor

Bridget: no, u have a good sense of humour. i like it .

BoBoy: well...

Bridget: i like u too

BoBoy: excuse me?

Bridget: oh blimey. did i say that?

BoBoy: um?

Bridget: i did. just forget it, all right?

BoBoy: oh gurl u are in trouble now ;-)

Bridget: it just slipped out. i was just thinking aloud sorry

BoBoy: really, it's ok

Bridget: i mean, i know u have a girlfriend and everything

BoBoy: slow down, bridge

Bridget: how embarrassing. this happens 2 me all the time. i just blurt out whatever's on my mind. just blurt it out and everyone looks at me like i have 2 heads

BoBoy: bridget

Bridget: what?

BoBoy: it's ok

Bridget: really?

BoBoy: really

Bridget: thank u, beau. oh how embarrassing.
i'll be good now

BoBoy: not a problem

Bridget: i'm so tired

BoBoy: well, ok... er, oh

so why can't u sleep?

Bridget: if i knew that...

BoBoy: let me see—u had a fight with someone

Bridget: well, i did, sort of

BoBoy: i knew it. yr boyfriend?

Bridget: i wish. haven't seen him 4 ages

BoBoy: bet u miss him

Bridget: <sigh>

BoBoy: so who did u fight with? oh, i got it. yr best
friend. mmm, that's rough

Bridget: how did u do that?

BoBoy: huh? nothing 2 it.

Bridget: really??

BoBoy: gurl like u, it's always 1 of 3 things

Bridget: what 3?

BoBoy: 1. boyfriend, 2. best friend, 3. worst enemy

Bridget: not bad

BoBoy: what did u fight about?

Bridget: that's simple: she's impossible

BoBoy: :)

Bridget: seriously!

BoBoy: no really

Bridget: okok, it's complicated. but basically she thinks i'm after her boyfriend

BoBoy: yow. that's big time

Bridget: but i'm NOT

BoBoy: ur not

Bridget: no. i mean, i do like him, but i'm NOT trying 2 take him away

BoBoy: sure...

Bridget: u don't believe me?

BoBoy: well, it's just like, where would she get that idea?

Bridget: u know how girls r

BoBoy: i do?

Bridget: suspicious! nasty. competitive. mean

BoBoy: oh, that :)

Bridget: k. so i did talk 2 him, and i do like him, and i did say nice things

BoBoy: but aside from that, ur in the clear :-D

Bridget: oh, i'm gonna get u

BoBoy: lol. from england?

Bridget: i mean it, beau, she is totally out of line on this

BoBoy: i hear u

Bridget: she practically pushed me at him, anyway

BoBoy: huh?

Bridget: i shouldn't be telling u, but i'm so mad at her. see, we had this bet, and it was like, ok, she tries 2 take my boy and i try 2 take hers

BoBoy: no way

Bridget: yes way

BoBoy: girls do stuff like that?

Bridget: pay attn. YES. oh yes

BoBoy: but why? i mean, i know why guys would do it, but that's 2 obvious 4 words

Bridget: true. but girls, well, maybe just 2 find out if they can trust their boyfriends

BoBoy: aw man, that is so RUDE

Bridget: no, it's not that way. more like they really WANT him 2 behave, but they want 2 know 4 sure, too. they're just insecure or something

BoBoy: in some parallel universe, this must make sense

Bridget: why? it makes total sense 2 me

BoBoy: 2 hand him candy that u don't want him 2 eat?

Bridget: come on, he knows he can't

BoBoy: shouldn't

Bridget: whatever. he knows u don't touch what isn't yrs

BoBoy: yeah but what about human nature?

Bridget: look, if he's not a jerk, he'll resist the temptation. simple

BoBoy: so u want him to PROVE he's not a jerk

Bridget: right

BoBoy: only he doesn't know he's being tested

Bridget: well duh...

BoBoy: oh, man. u guys r tough

Bridget: why??

BoBoy: this is so cruel. no wonder u can't sleep. it's yr conscience, girl

Bridget: ouch. why r u being mean now?

BoBoy: i'm not. i'm just saying

Bridget: i shouldn't have told u

BoBoy: nah, come on

Bridget: well. if i'm so cruel, then u surely don't want 2 talk 2 me

BoBoy: what?

Bridget: i'll just be going. thanks 4 nothing

BoBoy: no, wait

Bridget: and maybe i don't like u after all

BoBoy: bridge, wait

BoBoy: bridget?

BoBoy: bridge, please

Bridget: what?

BoBoy: just stay. talk 2 me

Bridget: why should i?

BoBoy: because u need 2 talk. i can tell

Bridget: no. i'm too CRUEL. obviously not good enough 2 talk 2

BoBoy: ok, i'm sorry for saying cruel. please stay

Bridget: no ur not

BoBoy: anyway, i just said the test was cruel, not u personally

Bridget: that's a... technicality

BoBoy: come on. u can let me off on a technicality, can't u?

Bridget: why should i?

BoBoy: just this once

Bridget: say please

BoBoy: please please preeeeze

Bridget: :)

BoBoy: there, see. u do still like me!

Bridget: don't be so sure. i could be just playing u

BoBoy: tell me more about yr best friend

Bridget: what about her?

BoBoy: what's the best thing?

Bridget: oh... she's brilliant. everyone says so

BoBoy: that's good. but that's not why u like her

Bridget: well, not really. i like her because... she's just a really good friend

BoBoy: she understands u?

Bridget: duh

BoBoy: she's supportive

Bridget: true. except today

BoBoy: she's fun, loyal, laughs at yr jokes, listens good

Bridget: yeah...

BoBoy: she likes u

Bridget: usually. she hates me lately

BoBoy: come on, girl. that will pass. it's not the first fight u ever had

Bridget: i don't know. she's really mad

BoBoy: aw, how could she stay mad at u? ur a sweetie

Bridget: don't be nice to me

BoBoy: but u R. ur just the sweetest lil ol thang

Bridget: no, u think i'm cruel and heartless

BoBoy: seriously. i can tell these things. ur like the nicest girl i ever met

Bridget: don't say that

BoBoy: no, it's true

Bridget: stop

BoBoy: k, stopping...

k, what's the biggest difference between u and yr best friend?

Bridget: um? dunno. maybe control stuff

BoBoy: interesting

Bridget: i mean, well, she's way into being on top of things. everything perfect, top marks in school, people saying the right words, things coming out perfectly

BoBoy: she likes things under control

Bridget: right

BoBoy: and u?

Bridget: well, i just can't do it. maybe because she's smarter than me

BoBoy: ur no dummy, bridge

Bridget: i am, compared 2 her

BoBoy: whatever. anyway, control isn't so important 2 u?

Bridget: yeah. well, i don't love chaos, but there's a little something about being just on the edge

BoBoy: kind of exciting

Bridget: totally. like when... no, i can't tell u this

BoBoy: yes u can

Bridget: you'll laugh

BoBoy: i won't. promise

Bridget: u better not.

ok, like when ur kissing a guy and something fluttery happens down in yr chest?

BoBoy: something fluttery?

Bridget: and like yr eyes kind of roll back and u almost faint? and, i dunno, everything's moving, and there's nothing u can do, and it's a little scary but totally exciting all at the same time?

BoBoy: bridge, ur making me all hot over here :)

Bridget: i know. it's nice, huh? <sigh>

BoBoy: woof. whoever he is, u got a lucky boyfriend

Bridget: hmmmmm

BoBoy: what?

Bridget: well... he thinks i could be more passionate. that's what i hear

BoBoy: get out. when ur feeling like THAT?

Bridget: no, seriously, he's not getting the message

BoBoy: he said ur not passionate?

Bridget: somebody told me, sort of. one of his friends

BoBoy: what a doof!

Bridget: i must be doing something wrong

BoBoy: why do u say that?

Bridget: well, i, um. k, i do get all kinda shy and quiet

BoBoy: the shy and passionate type. yowza!

Bridget: don't make fun of me

BoBoy: i'm not, bridge. seriously

Bridget: i can't help it

BoBoy: no, it's great. really fine. really sweet

Bridget: but what do i do about him?

BoBoy: he's english?

Bridget: um, yeah, english

BoBoy: not a chance. english r clueless about luv

Bridget: lol

BoBoy: ok. well, we gotta figure out how 2 give him a clue

Bridget: i thought about writing him a letter

BoBoy: eeek, no, not that

Bridget: why??

BoBoy: not good. much better in person

Bridget: like talk about it? i could never

BoBoy: well, no. not exactly talk about it. more like... ok, here. let's pretend

Bridget: pretend what?

BoBoy: u and me, ok? pretend like i'm yr boyfriend

Bridget: really?

BoBoy: sure. i'm not that bad a kisser...

Bridget: lol

BoBoy: ok, so we're kissing madly. u with me?

Bridget: well... ok i guess

BoBoy: so we're smooching away, and ur starting 2 feel that fluttery thing

Bridget: k...

BoBoy: feeling it?

Bridget: maybe

BoBoy: only maybe? hmm. how bout if i kiss yr neck, like on the left, just under yr chin? hot little kisses...

Bridget: k look. u have 2 court me. u can't jump me like a loose football

BoBoy: <ahem> sorry miss. i got carried away

Bridget: <smile> i'll say 1 thing 4 u, beau. u do make me laugh. my boy doesn't do that

BoBoy: really? why not? easiest thing in the world...

Bridget: i dunno. he's really sweet, but the brainy serious type

BoBoy: got it

Bridget: i mean, i'm totally gone on him. don't get me wrong

BoBoy: except for the passion bit...

Bridget: and that is so unfair. i'm really all about passion

BoBoy: ok, so let's figure it out. how do i court u?

Bridget: say some nice things, 4 starters

BoBoy: like what?

Bridget: i dunno. he always says nice things, gentle things about like nature and poetry and stuff. he can be pretty romantic

BoBoy: aw man. i can't think of that stuff. i'm a bozo

Bridget: try. pretend

BoBoy: ok. ur right. i should definitely learn this. where's johnson when i need him?... k <ahem> ready?

Bridget: ready

BoBoy: o bridget, the moon is shining on u. and the moon will be shining on me, too. and it's like going 2 be shining on both of us 2nite

Bridget: time out

BoBoy: not great, huh?

Bridget: no, it's fine, but. k, this just reminds me that we r on different sides of the ocean. u have 2 pretend we're together

BoBoy: ah. right

Bridget: k, take my hand

BoBoy: nice hand

Bridget: thank u. anything else?

BoBoy: um, k. yr hand, when u touch my face

Bridget: what part of yr face?

BoBoy: when u touch my cheek, yr fingers r soft as... butterfly wings

Bridget: nice start. go on

BoBoy: i kiss the fingers

Bridget: 1 by 1?

BoBoy: 1 by 1, and they taste, um, like cream and summer peaches

Bridget: mmm. let's go somewhere... somewhere safe

BoBoy: what? oh right. let's c

Bridget: and call me angel

BoBoy: come with me, my angel. come with me where the trees will protect us. c their limbs reach down like arms around... er... around our true luv

Bridget: very nice

BoBoy: i think i read that somewhere

Bridget: mmm, it still counts. keep going

BoBoy: dang. this is hard. k

it's so quiet here in the, uh... safety of the trees. just the softest breeze moving the flowers

moving them gently as my fingers stroke through yr hair

yr, um, auburn hair

and the air is cool, but yr lips r warm and sweet

bridge?

bridget?

Bridget: hmm?

BoBoy: where'd u go?

Bridget: what? i'm here

BoBoy: i thought u got lost in the trees, dude

Bridget: :) no, i was here. u were doing great

BoBoy: hmm

Bridget: what?

BoBoy: does this happen with... him—the english dude i'm starting 2 hate?

Bridget: lol. u mean, like does he ever think i got lost?

BoBoy: in a way

Bridget: maybe sometimes

BoBoy: really. hmm, k, let's think. where r yr hands right now? in this pretend world, i mean

Bridget: dunno. on yr shoulders?

BoBoy: so u don't really notice? k, when u start 2 get that fluttery feeling, do u sort of leave yr body?

Bridget: more like i go inside and just feel everything. i don't really know what i'm doing

BoBoy: like fainting

Bridget: a little, yeah

BoBoy: and u get real quiet and just feel everything happening

Bridget: maybe. why?

BoBoy: hmm. now i don't want 2 tell u, because it might help u get along with him ;-)

Bridget: u r so totally in my clutches, southern boy...

BoBoy: i'm a goner. but see, what i know is that u don't need 2 be more passionate, bridge

Bridget: i don't?

BoBoy: not at all. what u need is just 2 let. him. know.

Bridget: but how?

BoBoy: well, it's not that tricky. first, u probably hold off the fainting feeling a little longer

Bridget: why?

BoBoy: well, so u can hold his face, stroke his hair

Bridget: oic. duh me

BoBoy: whisper and moan

Bridget: really???

BoBoy: totally. bite, scratch. anything, really. am i being too forward?

Bridget: no i get it. yeah, wow, ur right. that's what i need 2 do

BoBoy: actually, no, i take it back. u should go totally still. cross yr arms and go stiff as a board

Bridget: lol

BoBoy: then when he breaks up with u, call me first thing

Bridget: ur a sweet guy, beau. <sigh>

BoBoy: not really

Bridget: oh yes ur. and beau?

BoBoy: yes, ma'am?

Bridget: well. what if i break up with the english chap and come after u right now?

BoBoy: be still my heart :) but seriously, u know i'm spoken 4. i'm totally gone on this girl. plus, she'd flat kill me if she knew i'd been taking romance lessons from u

Bridget: lol. and giving me kissing lessons...

BoBoy: that, too. woof. u won't tell, will u?

Bridget: yr secret's safe.... but i'm a little bit serious, beau. i like u a lot. we could work

BoBoy: aw man. that's really too nice 4 words, bridge, but no can do

Bridget: don't forget i'm coming 2 the states in the fall

BoBoy: try and find me

Bridget: oh, i'll find u. and don't hide behind yr girlfriend, u poof

BoBoy: lol

Bridget: seriously though. u know what we could be

BoBoy: i do, but bridge, please. u gotta stop saying this stuff

Bridget: ur right. sorry

BoBoy: but it's nice.... really nice <sigh>

Bridget: <sigh> call me angel 1 more time?

CHAPTER 15

missing

THE DAWG HOUSE

JUNE 10 8:30 PM

chessman has entered

chessman: dude

BoBoy: yo, wattup?

chessman: hey, you haven't heard from tamra have you?

BoBoy: not a word, bro

chessman: yeah

BoBoy: u?

chessman: nah

BoBoy: what IS it with them?

chessman: really

BoBoy: i mean does a cell phone not work in freakin florida?

chessman: sure, but you can't use em in a hospital

BoBoy: yeah, it like imbues the machines or something

chessman: but don't they ever leave to eat?

BoBoy: zackly

chessman: yeah

BoBoy: i leave her voice mail... "miss u" "call me"...
i text her... "miss u" "call me"

chessman: really? me too

BoBoy: and what do we get back?

chessman: we get silence

BoBoy: we get squat

chessman: zackly

BoBoy: i'm starting 2 get tired of this

chessman: i saw annie at the video store

BoBoy: yeah?

chessman: she says she hasn't heard either

BoBoy: well that's something

chessman: i guess

BoBoy: this whole thing stinks

chessman: you're getting pissed aren't you?

BoBoy: nah... yeah... a little

chessman: what's a guy to do?

BoBoy: women...

chessman: can't live with em

BoBoy: can't shoot em

chessman: heh

BoBoy: don't want 2 be a johnson

chessman: mr. "summer love, perhaps"

BoBoy: though i gotta say it's tempting...

chessman: yeah, well, easy for a babe magnet
            to say

BoBoy: get real. the babes r after u. open yr eyes

chessman: lol. if i knew any babes personally,
            i wouldn't know what to say

BoBoy: dude, u work too hard. just say "hey, u got plans
            2nite? i'm dying to see XYZ movie." keep it casual.
            that's how i met T

chessman: really?

BoBoy: totally. then "wanna see it with me?" close the deal

chessman: "not if you were the last geek on
            earth..."

BoBoy: lol. then u say, yo, my friend beau tanner's going

chessman: excellent. exploit my football
            connection

BoBoy: use the network, my dawg

chessman: annie said she got one text from
            bliss's mom's phone

BoBoy: her mom's phone?

chessman: yeah, it was, like, our phones are
            still at the house; can you tell
            the guys?

BoBoy: right. they forgot their cell phones...

chessman: i know

BoBoy: both of them...

chessman: i know

BoBoy: and then they text annie instead of us

chessman: i know

BoBoy: it's a bogus story

chessman: maybe

BoBoy: no dude, it's bogus. it's off the bogosity meter

chessman: could be. but annie showed me
their phones. she's gotta mail them
down there

BoBoy: annie has their phones...

chessman: yep

BoBoy: bro, it's too hard 4 me 2 figure out,
but there's something going on here

chessman: you feeling something?

BoBoy: totally. hey, remember the time we all got busted
4 smoking in the boy's room?

chessman: what about it?

BoBoy: when bartolo caught us, remember what johnson said?

chessman: he said, "i wasn't smokin..."

BoBoy: "the room was full of smoke and i just breathed that
in..."

chessman: lol

BoBoy: THAT'S bogosity

chessman: not even bartolo could keep a
straight face

BoBoy: bogus like ms. T without her cell

chessman: or bliss. sure. i getcha

BoBoy: what else did annie say?

chessman: nothing really. like, don't worry, bliss's mom probably has her busy all the time. stuff like that

BoBoy: what? like her granny died? they're planning a funeral?

chessman: annie didn't know. she's sending the phones

BoBoy: dude, u know... it's like... if they wanted 2 go away 2 gurls-only camp for 3 weeks, why not just say so?

chessman: so you think they're lying?

BoBoy: i dunno.... nah. T doesn't lie

chessman: yeah, and why WOULD they?

BoBoy: right. so i dunno

chessman: well...

BoBoy: yeah

chessman: yeah...

BoBoy: hey, u got plans 2nite? i'm dying 2 do the chat room...

chessman: lol. get away, you slut

BoBoy: seriously. that tatiana's fierce, bro. what's it like having her hit on u?

chessman: don't look at me. i'm innocent

BoBoy: sure, u just breathed...

chessman: seriously, i don't need the trouble

BoBoy: u mean with bliss? the missing bliss?

chessman: sure. but also when tatiana comes here this fall... i dunno... i mean, i like her, but...

BoBoy: really? i can't wait 2 meet bridget

chessman: i dunno... i want to meet her
         and everything, but tatiana's...
         complicated

BoBoy: come on. u like complicated

chessman: yes, but... whoa

BoBoy: she's a challenge

chessman: that's the truth...

BoBoy: ur just not used 2 a woman who can keep up
       with u

chessman: more like a step ahead of me. but
         seriously, i don't think i can do
         the whole "cat's away" thing

BoBoy: like the johnson thing? sure. but how do we know
       the women aren't doing that?

chessman: but until we do know, can you see
         getting involved?

BoBoy: it's just online, bro

chessman: yeah but hooking up online probably
         counts

BoBoy: bliss and T will never pin it on us

chessman: how come?

BoBoy: seriously, how r they gonna find out?

chessman: i dunno.... things always get found
         out

BoBoy: know what i think, bro?

chessman: what?

BoBoy: i think ur just freaked because tatiana came on
       2 u

chessman: heh heh, that too...

BoBoy: lighten up, dawg. this could be good 4 u

chessman: yeah...

BoBoy: **it's summer. don't imbue trouble**

chessman: lol. sure. i could be making too
much of it

BoBoy: **zackly. lighten up**

chessman: will do. btw, when's your birthday?

BoBoy: **july 2. why?**

chessman: i'm going to get you a new
dictionary

CHAPTER 16
philosophy

JUNE 10 10:45 PM

alfonso has entered

alfonso: ok, nobody gets ahead of us this time. we r totally on top of it. gonna move these pinheads like puppets on a string. like pawns on a chessboard. mwaa ha ha!

except that mitch is the chessmaster. hmm. and beau is his knight enforcer. at my best, i could never...

but it's just a figure of speech. too much fretting about metaphors. jeeze, that tamra girl and her peaches. can't we enjoy a victimless word crime anymore? of course we can

gotta love her, though. what conviction, what willpower, what ferocity. i'm actually starting 2 see things her way then there's bliss, bless her little tea cup. who'd a thunk there was so much 2 her? not my type, but u know. credit where due

and annie dearest. if only if only if only. may i die in her arms—is that so much 2 ask? her massive, merciless, amazon arms. ahhhh... crunch

oh, i'm so hopeless. slapslapslap. thanks captain, i needed that

✉ IM from gothling

gothling: johnson, u weasel, u shlump, u nancy boy

alfonso: the voice of my beloved! btw, those epithets don't work together

gothling: why not? i like em

alfonso: sorry, not good. with weasel, u go with something sneaky and craven—2 match weasel. like, "johnson, u weasel, u serpent, u sycophant." see?

gothling: u show-off! "craven" and "sycophant"—2 words i don't know in 1 sentence! don't ever do that 2 a woman... not while she's insulting u

alfonso: i kneel before u. please 2 forgive

gothling: i think not. so r we ready 2 go? anyone there yet?

alfonso: i came early

gothling: wish i could watch

alfonso: yeah, well. da boyz would see u, duh... but i'll IM u with constant updates, dearest, sealed with a kiss

gothling: eww. where those lips have been. anyway, keep me posted. i'm just watching tube

EXCHANGE STUDENT ROOM **UNION HIGH SCHOOL**

JUNE 10 11:00 PM

Tatiana has entered

Tatiana:	i am the first one here tonight?
alfonso:	yes, ur. except for yrs truly
Tatiana:	evening, johnson
alfonso:	actually, i'm glad we have a moment. i wanted 2 apologize again for my thoughtlessness in the past
Tatiana:	you're fine, J. let it go. i should thank you for being a sport about the name. i was strung out—it makes me rude
alfonso:	not at all. i was thinking a moment ago how persuasive ur on all this
Tatiana:	persuasive
alfonso:	yes, quite. i catch myself seeing things more and more yr way. unexpected
Tatiana:	well. i don't know what to say. thanks, johnson.

chessman has entered

chessman: i'm alive, i'm alive. and i won't
disappear this time

alfonso: yo mitchie. welcome u geek-weasel, u snake.
if u slither off this time, u will pay thru yr beady
little eyes

chessman: lol. u do have a way, johnson. i
don't care what brittney says

Tatiana: mitchell, hallo

chessman: hey tatiana. everything ok with you?

Tatiana: i think so. for why do you ask?

chessman: the storm. i've been checking the
weather in the adriatic, and it
looks pretty fierce

Tatiana: right. yes, the storm

chessman: your family ok?

Tatiana: very fine. things may look worse on the
radar maps than here on the earth. is
that how you say? "on the earth"?

chessman: on the ground?

Tatiana: oh yes. ground. a funny word

chessman: wow. i'm glad. because they were
saying the power is out all over
greece and albania. i didn't really
expect to see you here

Tatiana: the power? i'm not sure i know this...

alfonso: he means electricity. mitch, she was just telling
me that the electric has been off and on all nite

chessman: oic

alfonso: it may cut out again at any time. tatiana,
we're all quite relieved that ur safe

Tatiana: how kind. yes my family are quite fine.
            and mitchell, it is so grand to think of
            you thinking of me. i am all smiling

chessman: aw, well...

Tatiana: i have told my family how good you
            are to me

alfonso: get out. yr mother and everyone? u told them
            about mitch?

Tatiana: mother, of course. father and brothers.
            all are quite hoping for me to meet a wealthy,
            handsome american to take me
            out their hands one day :)

alfonso: lol

chessman: heh. i hope you do too

Tatiana: it could be you, if you play the card properly
            ;-)

chessman: sadly, my friend, i've given up cards :-)

Tatiana: alas

BoBoy has entered

BoBoy: finally made it, yo

alfonso: bubba, there ur. we thought u were bailing
            on us 2nite

BoBoy: not me. just a busy evening. yo mitch. yo tatiana

chessman: hey

BoBoy: johnson behaving himself?

alfonso: tsk tsk, let's not go there

BoBoy: is bridget not here yet?

alfonso: haven't seen her

Tatiana: are you so worried that she would be missing?

BoBoy: oh not really. just asking

Tatiana: i should be jealous

alfonso: he's concerned about her. bridget is usually right on time

Tatiana: i see. pardon me for thinking one woman could handle a gang of young geese like you 3

alfonso: sweet. she's jealous that she'd have 2 share us

chessman: lol, tatiana

BoBoy: geese, i like that

📨 IM from alfonso

alfonso: tatiana—i mean, tamra. what's the trouble?

Ms.T: what do you mean?

alfonso: ur pissed. r u and bliss still fighting?

Ms.T: maybe

alfonso: have u spoken 2 each other since the other nite?

Ms.T: not so much

alfonso: oh, gurl, this is trouble

Ms.T: why?

EXCHANGE STUDENT ROOM **UNION HIGH SCHOOL**

alfonso: know what, beau? do u mind buzzing bridget? just 2 see if she's home

BoBoy: sure. can do

Tatiana: oh, fine. go and chase the english

📨 IM from alfonso

alfonso: T, listen. u need 2 let go. i know it isn't easy

Ms.T: let go? i don't need to let her shag my boyfriend

alfonso: she's only playing a role. just like ur

Ms.T: i think she's doing more than that

alfonso: i REALLY don't agree. she's yr best best best friend, and u can trust her

Ms.T: like you would know about trust

alfonso: ???

Ms T: i'm sorry, johnson. that was totally out of line, and you've been so nice to me

alfonso: ur fine

Ms.T: seriously, i'm sorry. i know i'm too mad. i know it. and i know it isn't her fault, but it's getting out of hand. i just hate not having good options. i think i want out

alfonso: not good, T. u don't wanna do that

Ms.T: yes, i think i do. i'm miserable

alfonso: ok, but look. if u get out, that means cancel the whole game, lose the bet 2 annie, and fess up 2 da boyz. u want that?

Ms.T: why is that the only way? i could just have the power go out in albania. oh! oh! it's flickering right now!

alfonso: whatever. i'm not here 2 argue. but c, if the power goes out, then annie comes in with her magic wand and lights up everything. presto—u become a loser, and da boyz get away scott-free

Ms.T: arrgh

alfonso: u can do this T. i know u can. just play it out

Ms.T: double arrgh

alfonso: that's the spirit. buck up, soldier. and hey...

Ms.T: what?

alfonso: there's a great way to get revenge on bliss... and on beau

Ms.T: i know i know i know. I KNOW. but really. oh, ARRRRRGH. puff puff. ok, sarge, i'm going back in!

alfonso: that's it. go get em, gurl

⧉ IM from BoBoy

BoBoy: bridget? hello good evening?

Bridget: oh goodness, it's u

BoBoy: hey gurl, what up? u coming 2 the chat room?

Bridget: i dunno. i'm scared

BoBoy: really? scared of what?

BoBoy: bridget?

BoBoy: bridge? u still there?

Bridget: beau, i can't. i just can't. goodbye

Bridget is offline

BoBoy: bridge?

EXCHANGE STUDENT ROOM **UNION HIGH SCHOOL**

Tatiana: mitchell, i have question for you

chessman: fire away

Tatiana: what did your friend beau mean about "is johnson behaving himself"?

alfonso: tatiana, he was just messing with me. pay no attention

chessman: yeah, he was just kidding around

Tatiana: i don't believe you, mitchell. you are hiding something

chessman: well...

Tatiana: tatiana can tell when her darling is not saying truth

alfonso: oh dear oh dear oh dear

Tatiana: speak to me, mitchell. you know
i will find it

alfonso: u 2 have been chatting on the side, haven't u?

chessman: tatiana, it was really something
between me and beau and johnson.
i wouldn't be comfortable sharing
that without johnson's ok

Tatiana: it is about what we discussed? about
the horse?

alfonso: u can tell her, dude. she'll find out anyway

chessman: um, yeah. about that kind of stuff

Tatiana: i knew it! oh, mitchell, it is so thrilling
that you are my champion in america.
i am cover you with kisses. mwaa!

alfonso: man, this is 1 passionate chick. i mean,
woman. sorry?

BoBoy: well, group. bridget's not coming

Tatiana: really?

alfonso: what did she say?

BoBoy: said she's not coming. scared of something

alfonso: scared?

Tatiana: scared of what?

BoBoy: she wouldn't tell me. she's totally imbued

alfonso: come on! scared isn't gonna work. u can't
leave it there!!

Tatiana: please to excuse... my grandmama
calls in next room

alfonso: and dude?... imbued REALLY DOESN'T
MEAN WHAT U THINK IT DOES

chessman: oh let it go, johnson

alfonso: NOR CONTUMELIOUS! ALMOST NOTHING MEANS WHAT U THINK!!!

BoBoy: what i say? what i say?

chessman: johnson, chill. take a mozart pill

alfonso: arrrrgggghh. where's my pistol?

✉ IM from Ms.T

Ms.T: bliss taylor, you come out here this minute

bliss4u: shove off. u don't even like me

Ms.T: girl, i do too like you

bliss4u: go away!

Ms.T: you are my best best best friend

bliss4u: i'm leaving now

Ms.T: and i am here to apologize and grovel and whatever it takes

bliss4u: what's grovel? i don't know because i'm a MORON

Ms.T: it's begging, okay? i'm begging

bliss4u: begging is good...

Ms.T: bliss, i'm sorry. i was rude and angry and unfair. it was my fault entirely.

bliss4u: yes, that sounds like how i remember it

Ms.T: i'm sorry i'm sorry i'm sorry i'm sorry

bliss4u: well... u were mad about politics. that always gets u going

Ms.T: yes, and... to be more painfully honest, i was jealous

bliss4u: jealous

Ms.T: of you and Beau? helloo...

bliss4u: no way

Ms.T: oh gimme a BREAK. he totally likes you. i'm dying here

bliss4u: u think he likes me?

Ms.T: YES! the little slut puppy. i am SO going to make him pay when i get back to town

---

EXCHANGE STUDENT ROOM UNION HIGH SCHOOL

chessman: why are you all over bo? you think he can really make her come back??

alfonso: he's the only 1 with a shot

chessman: maybe she needs a night off. where's the harm?

alfonso: no, she's gotta be here. what did she say exactly, bubba?

 TXT to Johnson

June 10 11:28 pm
From: Gothling
yo J. ne thng gd?

TXT to gothling

June 10 11:30 pm
From: Johnson
crazy. will IM u in a min

EXCHANGE STUDENT ROOM **UNION HIGH SCHOOL**

BoBoy: she said "no way. i'm scared."
something like that

chessman: scared? i wonder what she's afraid of

BoBoy: she wouldn't talk about it

alfonso: aaarggggggghhh

BoBoy: NOW what? this guy is totally off his nut

chessman: it's his new leaf getting to him.
he's just not used to it

✉ IM from Ms.T

Ms.T: and worse than that, mitch is like impervious.

bliss4u: that's good, right?

Ms.T: for you, maybe. i'm totally throwing myself at him,
and he's all um, that makes me uncomfortable, tatiana...

bliss4u: true luv. it's a beautiful thing

Ms.T: that's what i thought, and now look at me. i've turned into a harpy

bliss4u: oh honey. it'll be ok...

Ms.T: whatever. so you coming back?

bliss4u: i guess. sure

Ms.T: wait. i'll tell them to send beau again.

bliss4u: let him talk me into it?

Ms.T: that would be the general idea

bliss4u: hee hee. i'm such a player. bye

Ms.T: i will kill that boy

EXCHANGE STUDENT ROOM **UNION HIGH SCHOOL**

Tatiana: beau, perhap you should try again with the english. you were maybe not the man enough last time, lol?

BoBoy: **not man enough?**

Tatiana: you know. maybe the little stronger persuasion

BoBoy: **what should i say?**

Tatiana: say anything! slap her around, no?

chessman: she's kidding

Tatiana: sorry, not myself today. no slapping

✉ IM from alfonso

alfonso: rough night, peaches

gothling: what's rough?

alfonso: the women. they've gone all random on me

gothling: i'll talk 2 them

alfonso: no, u stay out

gothling: johnson, i'll talk 2 them

alfonso: it's under control. a natural phase they're going thru

gothling: what phase?

alfonso: i think it's called "i hate my best friend because i let her snog my boyfriend." u know that phase

gothling: not personally

alfonso: funny, that's not how i heard it...

gothling: don't push it, reptile boy. i know where u live

EXCHANGE STUDENT ROOM **UNION HIGH SCHOOL**

BoBoy: so i should like tell her she's being a baby?

Tatiana: oh, american men. have you no finesse?

chessman: be european, beau. threaten
           suicide ;-)

Tatiana: ah, well. an operatic gesture.
           but i was thinking simpler

BoBoy: like what?

Tatiana: make it personal! tell her YOU need
           her to come back. not the group, but you

BoBoy: really?

Tatiana: is true, is it not? you want to see her

BoBoy: um? i guess so

Tatiana: ach, you swine

BoBoy: excuse me?

chessman: rotfl. you dog! hyena!

Tatiana: mitchell, my darling. only you understand
           these thing. YOU must go to the english and
           bring her by the hand

chessman: me?

BoBoy: no, that's kewl. i'll give it another shot

Tatiana: there, you see? the boy beau loves her,
           not me at all

chessman: are you really jealous, tatiana?

Tatiana: mitchell, i am so alone in this world. to
           lose any chance at love is more than i
           can bear sometime

chessman: i'm sure you have many chances

Tatiana: if you will not look at me fondly, then i
           am truly to die alone

✉ IM from alfonso

alfonso: listen, annabelle. let me be very serious with u

gothling: this should be good

alfonso: remember what u said 2 me about britt?

gothling: i said u were wasting yrself

alfonso: zackly. and i felt that way about u— with what's-his-name

gothling: voldemort

alfonso: u were wasted on him, annie

gothling: hmmph

alfonso: ur so much more of a woman than he could ever appreciate. u have depth that he will never know or understand

gothling: whatever

alfonso: i want u 2 find a man who can sing yr worth 2 the stars

gothling: i suppose u have someone in mind?

alfonso: i might. do u have someone in mind 4 me?

annie?

annie, don't hide from me

gothling: ur way over the line, johnson. we'll discuss it later

alfonso: as u wish. <sigh>

chessman: tatiana, do u think beau really
likes bridget?

Tatiana: but of course. see how he jump when
i told YOU to talk to her?

chessman: true

Tatiana: is it a problem if he does?

chessman: well, it could be. he's got a
girlfriend. a nice one

Tatiana: yes, racehorse girl

chessman: but he and bridget are only
friends online. so maybe that's ok

Tatiana: no, it is NOT ok

chessman: but i mean they can't do anything,
even if they do start to like
each other

📧 IM from BoBoy

BoBoy: it's me again. angel?

Bridget: oh, it's u. i was hoping u would come back
<sigh>

BoBoy: u were?

Bridget: bo, u have no idea how confused i am

BoBoy: ur?

Bridget: yes. i just can't get a grip

BoBoy: i'm sorry

Bridget: don't be sorry. it's not yr fault

BoBoy: oh. whew :)

Bridget: well, yes it is. in a way

BoBoy: no fair. how is it my fault?

Bridget: let's not talk about this now. we should go 2 the chat room

BoBoy: great. u changed yr mind

Bridget: i guess

BoBoy: everyone wants u 2 come

Bridget: everyone? what about u?

BoBoy: um? yes. me too

Bridget: just me too?

BoBoy: ok... me, most of all

Bridget: i'm blushing

BoBoy: take my hand. let's go back

EXCHANGE STUDENT ROOM **UNION HIGH SCHOOL**

Tatiana: can't do anything online? can they not fall in love?

chessman: i guess. but is that the same?
it's not like they can hook up in
real life

Tatiana: tell me, darling mitchell. you are such the
philosopher. would the girlfriend of beau
feel this way? that falling in love online is
not real life?

chessman: hmm. true

Tatiana: is love not real when it is online?

chessman: i guess it is

Tatiana: you are honest man. and this is why
you resist me so strongly, yes? because you
know online is real life too

chessman: i see you've thought this through

Tatiana: i think of nothing else since i meet you,
and that is the gods' truth

alfonso: well, what have we here? a regular coffee klatsch

chessman: yeah, kind of a philosophical
discussion i guess

BoBoy: hey hey. guess who came back with me

Bridget has entered

alfonso: excellent! we were so out of balance without u,
bridget

Tatiana: hallo hallo, darling. i am so happy you
are here

Bridget: well, ur a peach 2 say so, tatiana

BoBoy: uh oh

Tatiana: lol, pumpkin

alfonso: whew. i thought we were in trouble there

Tatiana: i laugh only because i don't know how to swear in english

alfonso: oh, mitch can give you private lessons when you get 2 america

Bridget: i'm sure mitchell doesn't curse ;-)

Tatiana: bridget darling, one question

Bridget: yes, girlfriend?

Tatiana: pumpkins are round and fat, are they not?

CHAPTER 17
suicide

GURLGANG ROOM

JUNE 11 5:20 PM

gothling: **seems like yr boy beau has his mind on england an awful lot, heh heh. u ready 2 concede the bet?**

Ms.T: his mind wanders. big deal

gothling: **it will be l8r**

bliss4u: if annie wants 2 quit now, let's do, so we win! i'm desperate 2 get mitchie back

gothling: **not a chance**

Ms.T: so what are you saying, bliss? you tired of beau already? you hussy ;-)

bliss4u: funny thing is, i never expected 2 like him, but he's awesome. really really nice. i mean, i like him as bridget, of course... he makes me laugh

Ms.T:	he IS awesome, but i'm so disappointed in him. i thought he'd see right through you. funny or not, he's a chump
gothling:	**told ya**
Ms.T:	i could snatch him bald-headed
bliss4u:	well, wait. he isn't like madly in love or anything. nothing unforgivable. he's only being nice
gothling:	**oh it still counts. she can kill him anytime now**
Ms.T:	actually no, bliss is right. let's not be in contumelious haste
bliss4u:	lol. he is so cute when he says stuff like that
Ms.T:	i know. awww. i hate him
gothling:	**k, come on. what's he actually saying 2 bridget? give us the goods**
bliss4u:	i blush 2 repeat...
Ms.T:	whatever
bliss4u:	well... k, here's 1 strange thing that happened. i was actually all worried about tatiana—being such a passionate bee-yotch and all? and thinking that mitch was so unhappy with me
gothling:	**oh, yeah. "maybe he'd like a little spanking." that stuff. the strong woman stuff**
bliss4u:	c, and that's u and tam. i am totally not like that. so i got all worried that mitchie thought i was not, u know, passionate
Ms.T:	darling, your mitchell is utterly devoted. i will never break him down
bliss4u:	<sigh> but anyway, so i have bridget say 2 beau that her boyfriend in england thinks the same thing—like "oh, his friend told me that he thinks i'm cold, whatever will i do?" and stuff like that

gothling:	gurl, nice work. play the sympathy card why dontcha?
Ms.T:	it works every time on that bozo. jeeze. <slap my worried brow>
bliss4u:	it DOES work on him! i luv that. oh, and he's all, how awful, what could be wrong? like he wants 2 fix everything so i'll be happy with my boyfriend again. it's sweet, tam. ur so lucky
Ms.T:	grrrr. and i was mad that he has bridget in his buddy list
bliss4u:	but k, so bridget's boyfriend—beau calls him "that english dude i'm starting to hate." lol
Ms.T:	oh very cute. shut up, annie. i can hear you laughing
bliss4u:	anyway, so i sorta tell him how it goes when we're making out and stuff. and i'm, like, now why would he think i'm cold??
gothling:	wait. really? how DOES it go?
bliss4u:	ooo, i get all fluttery inside and everything. like i nearly pass out every time. it's totally exciting
gothling:	so i don't get it
bliss4u:	no, c, that's the problem. i'm all trembly and quiet, so mitchie thinks i don't like it when i totally do.
Ms.T:	<groan> so now you get advice from beau on how to snog with mitchell
bliss4u:	yeah. heh. so he says ok, basically, to fight off the fluttery stuff... just do anything...
Ms.T:	do anything...
bliss4u:	be wild. scratch him, bite him, whisper and moan and carry on like. so he knows! THEN u can pass out

Ms.T: oh jeeze oh jeeze oh pete <sigh>

bliss4u: nice, huh? i'm gonna try it

gothling: **i wonder where he came up with those ideas... any theories, ms. T?**

Ms.T: i'll just be going now. i have an appointment with mr. death

bliss4u: what?

gothling: **lol. and really, such excellent advice: whisper, moan... bite & scratch**

bliss4u: oh no... u mean...

gothling: **rotfl. let me catch my breath**

bliss4u: how embarrassing. i'm sorry, tam

Ms.T: bliss, you've met my former friend annie, haven't you?

gothling: **whew. that was wonderful**

Ms.T: i plan to kill her right after i kill myself

bliss4u: i am so sorry, tam

gothling: **okokokok**

bliss4u: i had no clue

gothling: **so bubba is indiscreet but basically harmless. how about the nerd patrol? what u got, tam?**

Ms.T: <sigh sigh sigh> nothing. abso-bloody-lutely nothing. mitchell is the soul of devotion to his girl. i would despise him if he weren't so freakin cute about it all

gothling: **oh, get a grip, camper. there must be something**

bliss4u: no, i'm ok just how she left it =)

Ms.T: there must be something? ok: he's willing to be my "friend"—tatiana's friend. how's that? pretty juicy, huh?

gothling: **there's more, or ur not trying**

Ms.T: arrgh. let me think. ok i know he LIKES tatiana. he follows the weather in albania. reads up on the history and everything. i'm on the web all the time just trying to stay ahead of him. but it's SO far from romance. it's like a really interesting homework assignment to him

bliss4u: no that sounds just like mitchie. he's the most sincere guy i've ever met

Ms.T: i hate him.... actually, no. now don't get me wrong bliss, but i could totally see it working with mitch. he's got stuff going on

bliss4u: stuff?

Ms.T: you should know. it's like i've only seen the surface of mitch before. that boy has soul... but that's probably why i can't budge him off his gurl....

gothling: **come on. u gotta lead him on. where's yr womanly wiles??**

Ms.T: i DO lead him on. i flirt shamelessly. i order him around. i make him apologize for his friends. i call him darling. i pout. i whine. i abuse him. i sweet-talk him. <sigh> nothing. nothing. i'm a failure as a woman

bliss4u: oh, sweetie

Ms.T: i'm nothing compared to bliss. is it all because you have bigger pompoms?

bliss4u: lol

gothling: **there must be some way 2 get at him. did u try helpless? lonely?**

Ms.T: he helps. he talks. that's it

gothling: **the direct approach?**

Ms.T: i was passionate, alluring, i was poetic

gothling:	**hmmm**
Ms.T:	haven't tried terminal illness...
gothling:	**ahhh. k, how bout suicide?**
Ms.T:	excuse me???
gothling:	**suicide. it's worth a try**
bliss4u:	oh that is totally unfair
gothling:	**drastic measures are called 4**
Ms.T:	couldn't i just get a tumor?
gothling:	**suicide suicide**
bliss4u:	no way
gothling:	**u know he won't let u jump off an albanian cliff**
Ms.T:	that's just humiliating
gothling:	**even halfway round the world, it's gotta work**
bliss4u:	so obvious
Ms.T:	really
gothling:	**i'm not hearing better ideas...**
bliss4u:	come on! it is totally not fair. mitchie would freak. he would die of hurt
gothling:	**i rest my case**
Ms.T:	interesting
bliss4u:	arrrrgh. u people
Ms.T:	very interesting
bliss4u:	besides, tatiana would never pull a stunt like that. threaten suicide?? are u kidding?
Ms.T:	tatiana is feel so alone right now. she say this very thing to mitchell...

bliss4u: don't call him that

gothling: **she's vulnerable**

Ms.T: she's lonely. so lonely

bliss4u: but but... she has a boyfriend

Ms.T: actually, he's away right now. and you know italian men...

bliss4u: ackack

gothling: **so she's desperate. yes, and this sincere american boy is all that stands between her and certain death by a broken heart**

bliss4u: ur so twisted

gothling: **why?**

bliss4u: because it's cheating. and tatiana isn't shameless and weak like that

gothling: **why can't she be? bridget's a ho. who'd a predicted that?**

bliss4u: shut up, annie

Ms.T: oh now u insulted bridget

gothling: **why is she mad? it's only a character**

bliss4u: bridget is not ONLY a character

gothling: **r u losing yr mind? i do not get this girl**

bliss4u: she's MY character, and she's not a ho

Ms.T: well, but she IS after my beau

bliss4u: my character. my creation. not like some mask i'll throw away when i'm tired of her

gothling: **oh dear oh dear**

bliss4u: i LIKE her. i made her and i like her

Ms.T: i know, bliss

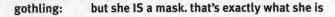

gothling: **but she IS a mask. that's exactly what she is**

bliss4u: annie can't feel like this about her uncle jerry whozit, the scout leader preacher card-reader redneck from maryland

gothling: **minnesota**

bliss4u: and that's nobody's fault but yr own. if u weren't so repressed, maybe u could luv someone too

Ms.T: whoa whoa. time out sister

gothling: **whatever. i didn't know she could type this fast**

bliss4u: so frigid

Ms.T: ok, kids, let's don't go there

gothling: **actually i'm pleased that she knows the word "repressed"**

Ms.T: annie, chill

gothling: **what?**

Ms.T: you're getting your iron vest on. there's no need

bliss4u: i can MAKE her a ho, if that's what everyone wants

Ms.T: nobody wants that, bliss

bliss4u: bridget, u a bitch ho

what? no, i most certainly am not

yes. they say u a english ho now

k, if i a ho, i better shake this booty all up in that bubba face

gothling: **gurl, that is SO bad**

Ms.T: bridget, would u go back 2 being a nice english girl?

bliss4u: make up yr mind

Ms.T: we were just talking about getting to mitch.
if you don't like suicide, we have to think of
something else

bliss4u: why doesn't annie just admit that mitch is
not gettable, and we call it a day?

**gothling: look, prissy, u agreed to the terms. u put yrself in
my hands 2 c if u can trust him. u can't just rule out
anything that makes u feel threatened**

bliss4u: but this is an unfair trick

gothling: so u don't trust him after all?

Ms.T: ok, whatever. how about this... bliss doesn't
get to rule out anything, but i'm not saying i'll
do it either

gothling: oh, gurl, u don't have a chance without it

Ms.T: there's lots we haven't tried. i'll work on it

**gothling: look, i'm calling the shots here. u guys agreed
2 this**

Ms.T: let's ask johnson

bliss4u: what?

Ms.T: let's ask johnson. he'll have ideas

gothling: hmm. i'm feeling chilly toward johnson right now

bliss4u: actually, that's not a bad idea

Ms.T: it's a great idea. i'll go talk to him

gothling: wait a minute

bliss4u: we'll both go, if annie's mad at him

**gothling: just settle down. i'll talk 2 johnson. u lil campers
aren't cut out 4 this**

bliss4u: we can all talk 2 him

gothling: I'LL do it, and i'll do it alone. he's not 2 be trusted with u

Ms.T: whatever

gothling: but no guarantees

bliss4u: sure, but why can't we all go?

gothling: and if he says suicide, then that's it. understood?

Ms.T: suits me

bliss4u: he won't. i know he won't like the suicide idea

gothling: we'll just see what he says. but remember, i'm still in charge

CHAPTER 18
wounds

✉ IM from gothling

JUNE 11 7:09 PM

gothling: johnson, we have 2 talk

alfonso: at yr service, miss. as always

gothling: tamra's running out of steam with the chessman. u gotta do something

alfonso: but lovey, why me?

gothling: dude, i thought u were like this grand puppeteer

alfonso: i can't work miracles

gothling: u were this colossus, this wizard of the heart

alfonso: if yr puppet has no imagination, it's hardly my fault

gothling: the fault is with YR puppet, pal, not mine

alfonso: lil mitchie-poo? what's he done?

gothling: nothing! that's the problem!

alfonso: well, what has she tried?

gothling: everything

alfonso: flirtation?

gothling: constantly

alfonso: humor? despair?

gothling: yes...

alfonso: wit? abuse? helplessness?

gothling: been there, done those

alfonso: mystery? lechery?

gothling: everything, johnson

alfonso: oh mitchell <sigh>

gothling: he has 2 get with the program

alfonso: sad sad sad. and tatiana is such a fox, too. such a mezzo

gothling: i know! isn't she great?

alfonso: the passion, the bad accent, the brazen flirting

gothling: the lurking sadness

alfonso: well, u can't really say "lurking" with "sadness"

gothling: lurk is what i said. her sadness lurks

alfonso: it does, eh? hmm

gothling: behind her bright exterior lurks a gloomy, gloomy... gloom

alfonso: well, sadness doesn't lurk, but k, yes, she's been seriously dark. hmm, yeah. we could work with that

gothling: good, but how?

alfonso: u know what? tell her 2 go all gypsy on him!

gothling: all gypsy?

alfonso: gurl, it's perfect. darkness and destiny, passion and pulchritude.... oh! OH! get her reading the cards 4 him

gothling: kewl. yes. great idea

alfonso: ach. no! not for him—how silly of me—4 HERSELF

gothling: u lost me there

alfonso: k, the source of her foreboding, her enclosing (not lurking) sadness, the source EVEN of her passion 4 life, lurks (lurks!) within the dark clouds of her own destiny. a destiny that she reads... where, gypsy gurl?

gothling: oh i like...

alfonso: u see? i do have 1 or 2 things going 4 me

gothling: ur a surprising guy, johnson. i won't deny it

alfonso: and i'll work on mitch. he needs some prep 4 this. i'll have to accidentally know something about tatiana

gothling: some dark secret?

alfonso: some dark and terrible secret

gothling: some dark terrible operatic secret?

alfonso: destiny is unjust... yes, i can totally get mitch going with this.... plus the whole card thing. keep it vague and dark. yeah. mitch will buy this

gothling: if he doesn't, we're going 4 suicide

alfonso: oh, please. like what? "say u love me, or i kill myself"?

gothling: what's wrong with that?

alfonso: it's not terribly inventive, is it?

gothling: well, if he's too dense 2 go 4 yr pretty stories, we have 2 give him something blunt and obvious

alfonso: sure. k whatever.

but annabelle... i mean...

suppose he does understand, but he's just totally committed to bliss? think about it. kinda sweet in a way

gothling: impossible

alfonso: u don't know men

gothling: yes, i do

alfonso: <gurgle> scuse me while i count to 10... k. annie dear?

gothling: what?

alfonso: k, yes u do. u know a great deal about men. about women too. but sometimes there r matches that just work. they just do

gothling: oh please

alfonso: i know it's corny, i know it's old-fashioned, but some people r willing 2 pass up all offers and save their hearts 4 that special someone

gothling: johnson, that's romantic hogwash. guys r all alike. they're all horn dawgs. just like u, dear, only not as honest

alfonso: i'm telling u. even guys like me would give it all up 4 the girl of their dreams

gothling: u can't ask a compass not 2 point north

alfonso: annabelle, u know SO much about the heart. but ur counting a lot on 1 bad experience

gothling: darling. sweetie. sweetie darling: shut up

alfonso: my word as an opera buff. it's possible 2 dwell too long on 1 tragedy

gothling: johnson, let's don't, k?

alfonso: annie, what he did 2 u, what she did—that doesn't have 2 ruin yr life

gothling: we r not talking about this

alfonso: doll, u need 2 talk

gothling: no. she was my best friend, johnson, got it? if u HAD any friends u would understand

alfonso: i know i know. but annie, maybe it's time 2 try again

gothling: we are NOT talking about it, johnson. ur way over the line, u hear me?

alfonso: <sigh>

gothling: finish about mitch. then i'm going

alfonso: ah yes, mitch! said johnson, closing the wound, fixing his tie...

gothling: j-man, don't do this, bro...

alfonso: so mitch! the pitch 2 mitch. mitch needs a pitch. mitch needs a picture, actually. let's paint him something plain. something he can see without his glasses

gothling: yeah, he's not totally clear on the mysteries of luv

alfonso: unlike u and me, right?

gothling: stop it

alfonso: well, not 2 worry. i'll take care of it. he needs more opera in his life. but hey, beau told me some very interesting stuff

gothling: what?

alfonso: turns out bridget's "english" boyfriend can woo her quite well. she told beau all about it

gothling: like what?

alfonso: like, oh, how about:

>   come away my dove, and
>   let us seek the loving trees,
>   where breeze and blossom will conspire
>   to take our passion higher and higher.

not as good as that, because that's 1 of mine. but the point is, ol' mitch is a romantic. who'd'a thunk?

gothling: gag me. that was like a glass of syrup

alfonso: really? that was from the poem i promised u. nature, elegance, nice internal rhymes? not?

gothling: i'm thinking not

alfonso: rats. i spent 6 whole minutes on that

gothling: johnson, now that wounds ME. it's not that i totally WANT yr attention, but i'd like 2 believe i'm worth more than 6 MEASLY MINUTES OF A HIGH SCHOOL POET'S TIME

alfonso: annabelle, my sweet...

gothling: what?

alfonso: ur worth a whole lifetime of high school poetry

CHAPTER 19
mediterranean

THE DAWG HOUSE
JUNE 13 9:00 PM

BoBoy: yo mitch

chessman: zup?

BoBoy: nothin really

chessman: yeah me too

BoBoy: u heard from bliss?

chessman: i wish

BoBoy: me too

chessman: i dunno

BoBoy: what?

chessman: nah. well

ok, sometimes i wonder if this
could actually be her way of breaking
up? like she couldn't tell me to
my face, but she maybe wants to see
other people. i dunno

BoBoy: **so she just goes away**

chessman: i guess

BoBoy: **yeah**

chessman: but i don't really think it's true

BoBoy: **no**

chessman: just wonder sometimes

BoBoy: **me too. i get a bad feeling about it sometimes**

chessman: but dude, ms. T would tell u
straight out if she wants to see
other people. she would do that

BoBoy: **so why doesn't she?**

chessman: zackly. why?

BoBoy: **right**

chessman: so, in a way, that's good

BoBoy: **it's good that she doesn't tell me?**

chessman: because you know if she had
something to say, she'd say it

BoBoy: **what? oh. which totally means she doesn't feel
like that**

chessman: because she hasn't told you

BoBoy: **that's brilliant, debater dude**

chessman: well, it's an argument from silence,
but it's all we've got right now

alfonso has entered

alfonso: word up, dudes

chessman: zup J?

BoBoy: **word**

alfonso: gentlemen, u will be pleased 2 hear that i am totally getting used 2 this single dude status

chessman: seriously?

alfonso: (which u so unkindly imposed without my consent—and don't think i'll ever forget it)

BoBoy: **ur liking it? get real**

alfonso: no, i mean it. best thing i've ever done. i am feeling... what's the word... purged, i guess

BoBoy: **purged**

alfonso: purged of unwanted karma. i am totally finding myself—who i am, what i need, what i don't need

chessman: who'd a thunk it? so what don't you need?

alfonso: women! the need is gone

chessman: get real

alfonso: i feel like 1 of those old dudes who go 2 the desert 2 live in a hole or something

BoBoy: **a hermit**

alfonso: zackly. they like sit in a cave all naked and don't talk 2 anyone. stay alive on bugs and pure thoughts

chessman: subsistence living

BoBoy: **kewl. so have u subsided now?**

alfonso: um?

BoBoy: **that's beautiful, J**

chessman: but, johnson, you talk to people.
you eat. you don't meditate. you're
no desert monk

alfonso: that's not the point, nerdman.
even without all that, u boys have put me on the
edge, the very edge, of privation

chessman: oic. you're deprived of women.
well, that's cool. a sacrifice

BoBoy: wow. so yr mind is like razor sharp these days?

alfonso: i am experiencing clarity like never before

BoBoy: kewl. we shoulda thought of this a long time
ago, mitchie

alfonso: i'm also feeling compassion 4 others.
unexpected, truly

chessman: compassion! whoa. call a medic.
the boy is breaking down

BoBoy: compassion 4 who?

alfonso: well, i shouldn't...

chessman: oh, he's playing us

alfonso: nah. well, actually. k, i don't trust u, but it's annie

BoBoy: annie. i'm drawing a blank here, bro

alfonso: annie. i feel compassion 4 annie. duh??

chessman: i don't think beau knows annie's
story, J

BoBoy: what story?

alfonso: ah, now i c. sorry, dude. the new me is sorry

chessman: beau, the thing with annie is that
she had this boyfriend. i knew him
from somewhere. but he was totally
not right for her

BoBoy: but really, who would be?

alfonso: what do u mean? i can think of 1 or 2

BoBoy: dude, she's totally goth and totally butch at the same time. she's an azore... no, that thing on the web

chessman: an amazon

alfonso: aw, man, she is not

chessman: don't say she's a peach, J. that ain't gonna work here

alfonso: she's hurt, that's all. can't u see that?

BoBoy: she's hurt...

alfonso: totally. u don't know what that dude did 2 her

BoBoy: what?

chessman: oh, it was cold. i heard it from bliss

alfonso: zackly. well, i mean, she's not the first it's happened 2, but annie's like this tower of strength and self-control and... and...

BoBoy: know-it-all-ness

chessman: lol. she totally does know everything—just ask her

alfonso: yeah, yeah. accepting dissent is not her strength

BoBoy: does she even know what that is?

alfonso: fine. we know she's hardball. that goes without saying

chessman: and she's bitter. never a kind word these days

alfonso: all right, fair enough. she's brusque. that's the 1 thing u can say against her, but here's my point

BoBoy: and she like has 2 control the conversation. every conversation

alfonso: true, k

chessman: hostile?

BoBoy: defensive?

chessman: competitive

alfonso: okokok. so she's hardheaded. she's a little arrogant, hostile, defensive, controlling, bitter, and butch. but aside from that, what has annie ever done 2 us?

BoBoy: contumelious?

alfonso: oh, shut up, bubba

chessman: dude, i'm starting to think johnson likes annie

alfonso: compassion where compassion's DUE. that's what i'm trying 2 say

chessman: she was hurt bad

BoBoy: so what did the dude do 2 her?

chessman: bliss told me she swore off romance for a year

alfonso: what he did, my brother, was hook up with her best friend

BoBoy: what? that can't be legal...

chessman: totally over the line

alfonso: even i have never done that

BoBoy: her best friend. ouch. so that's why annie is worked all the time

chessman: i just don't tangle with her

alfonso: it's a touching story, don't u think? almost an opera

BoBoy:　　　**nobody's heartless here, J**

alfonso:　　　that's what i'm talking about. compassion where due

chessman:　　she's a human being too

BoBoy:　　　**glad to hear it**

chessman:　　johnson, you're really turning it over, aren't you? i have to say i'm surprised

alfonso:　　　i'm not too proud to admit it

chessman:　　but well, so have you sworn off women?

alfonso:　　　not totally, no. our deal is i'm free when the chat room is over. in the meanwhile, being the hermit is instructive. turns out i enjoy watching

BoBoy:　　　**yeah, i gotta try that sometime**

chessman:　　we're practically monks lately, anyway

BoBoy:　　　**lol. hey, johnson, 1 question. u don't think bliss and ms. T r trying to ditch us, do u?**

alfonso:　　　dude, u know as much as i do

chessman:　　so no news through annie, you're saying?

alfonso:　　　sometimes an absence is only an absence

BoBoy:　　　**seriously, what do u know?**

alfonso:　　　k, last i heard from annie was that bliss and tam were hoping to reappear, but no one knows when they'll make it

BoBoy:　　　**how come she can reach them and we can't?**

alfonso:　　　dude, u know women. they have ways

BoBoy:　　　**yeah**

alfonso:	but hey. speaking of women, have u heard from tatiana?
BoBoy:	not me. i'm the bozo, remember? mitch is da man
chessman:	oh right. what did you hear, johnson?
alfonso:	well, she wrote me something kinda dark
BoBoy:	what was it?
alfonso:	actually, i'm a little worried about her
BoBoy:	j-man, more compassion? now I'M worried
chessman:	seriously, what's she saying?
alfonso:	i don't know if u guys will totally believe me, because u think i have this like gothic imagination and stuff
chessman:	well, you do, but give us a try
alfonso:	altho i'm nothing compared 2 that girl's life
BoBoy:	sure
alfonso:	because she's like living in an opera, practically. u know how those people r
BoBoy:	what people?
chessman:	albanians
alfonso:	actually, i meant all cultures of the mediterranean region
chessman:	i stand corrected. please go on
alfonso:	how to begin?... k, as we know, in her country, there r the rich, there r the poor, and there r gypsies. and of course these groups never mix. so it is totally out of the question for a gypsy 2 aspire 2 riches. a poor man would never hope 2 court the baron's sister. and the daughter of a wealthy man may never, never—no matter how she loves him—marry a gypsy boy

BoBoy: **we know this?**

chessman: well, sort of. social classes
              are tougher in europe than they
              are over here. johnson is being
              dramatic, but yeah

alfonso: thank u 4 that overwhelming vote of confidence.
              now shut up.

              k, as fate would have it, tatiana comes from a
              well-to-do family. a very well-to-do family

BoBoy: **kewl. did we know this too?**

chessman: they're connected with oil or some
              kind of mineral exploration. she
              didn't say exactly

alfonso: point is, and much 2 her family's dismay, she's
              in love... with a gypsy

BoBoy: **no way! so that's like a death sentence, right? oh,**
              unfair unfair unfair

alfonso: the old ways are strong in her country. but
              now i tell u this with great sadness: she had
              thought the gypsy boyfriend went away 2 plan their
              elopement. she said something like this in
              the chat room

chessman: well, not exactly. but yeah, ok.
              he's in italy

alfonso: she was 2 meet him there in 6 months, and they
              would run away 2 where her family would never
              find them. very romantic, but totally the truth as
              she tells it

              but now, word has reached her that her
              gypsy love...

BoBoy: **what?**

alfonso: ...has died

BoBoy: i knew it

alfonso: he fell from a balcony—no, how did she say it?—from a rampart. in rome

chessman: you better not be jerking our chain, J

alfonso: u have seen my poor poems. do u think that in my wildest dreams i could write a story this sad?

BoBoy: true...

alfonso: and that's not all. at first she thought like her father had him killed, 2 keep them apart. but now, it looks like the dude saw how little hope there was, and...

BoBoy: what?

alfonso: well, tatiana thinks he may have... jumped

BoBoy: no way

chessman: seriously?

alfonso: tatiana doesn't let on. u know how strong she is. but i can tell she's beside herself with grief. and her family r beside themselves with shame. i mean, a gypsy with their own daughter. now a suicide, a daughter in despair. they think she might do something terrible

chessman: aw man, so that could explain...

alfonso: why they're sending her 2 america. u got it, dude

BoBoy: i knew it. i knew it

chessman: they want her to find an american boyfriend

alfonso: yeah, but mitch, who cares what they want?

chessman: i dunno. just thinking about something she said

alfonso: but who CARES about that? i'm afraid she'll do something 2 herself. she's so volatile, and she totally blames herself 4 his death

chessman: blames herself? how is this her fault?

BoBoy: aw man, this is terrible

alfonso: she's in a dark place, dudes. very dark

BoBoy: we gotta do something

alfonso: she keeps talking about the cards and all

chessman: the cards?

alfonso: u know, the cards. fortune-telling. gypsy stuff

chessman: really?

alfonso: dude, he was teaching her that stuff. how 2 see yr future and all. she thinks he maybe saw their future and that's why he jumped

chessman: aw man. this is too much

alfonso: now all she sees in the cards is death

BoBoy: yipe. mitch, u gotta do something

chessman: me?? i don't know what to do about stuff like this

alfonso: no, wait... bubba's right

chessman: no he's not

alfonso: tatiana does like u, man. she talks about u...

BoBoy: mitch, u gotta talk 2 her

alfonso: she trusts u. ur so stable

chessman: come on, what would i say to her???

BoBoy: nah, u don't talk about this stuff. just let her talk

alfonso: whatever she wants 2 talk about. just get her
             thru this rough patch...

chessman: just let her talk...

alfonso: u could lighten her load, mitch

BoBoy: u could save a life

alfonso: how many hopeless nerds can say that?

chessman: shove off, J

BoBoy: seriously, bro. me and johnson, we're just rednecks
             2 her

alfonso: totally

BoBoy: we'd probably call her a lamp or a truck or something

chessman: gimme a break

BoBoy: mitch, u gotta. it could be her life

alfonso: u know how impulsive she can be

chessman: but she's after me already, and
             i really can't be her american
             boyfriend

BoBoy: just 4 a while... get her thru this

chessman: no way. i can't pretend stuff like
             that

alfonso: no, ur right, dude: don't pretend anything.
             nobody's saying marry her

BoBoy: just listen 2 her

chessman: i could MAYBE just let her talk...

BoBoy: zackly

alfonso: ur solid, dude. ur a rock. that's all she needs...

chessman: i've got rocks in my head. that's
             what i've got

alfonso: aw, where's the compassion?

chessman: i KNOW, but what about bliss???

alfonso: dude, pleeeeze. some things r not about bliss!!

chessman: ....

alfonso: come on mitchie...

BoBoy: she's really imbued, yo...

chessman: <groan>

alfonso: just listen. that's all u have 2 do...

chessman: arrrgghh

BoBoy: just let her talk...

YOUR UNCLE JERRY'S BLOG

Marriage of the Minds
14 JUNE

> *Let me not to the marriage of true minds*
> *Admit impediments.*
> *—Shakespeare, lame old love sonnet*

Joy and peace, camper. Marriage is what brings us together. Marriage, that age-old, universally celebrated union between heart and heart, is not—pay attention, young feller—NOT to be taken lightly.

Why do young campers love to marry? Up here in Minnesota, where the lonesome wind blows in from the prairie, it is the opinion of certain older persons that marriage was invented so that everyone can stay warm through the winter. Ho ho. Your Uncle Jerry's own mother got engaged three times, just looking for a man who didn't have cold feet.

Your Uncle Jerry himself will never marry. Uncle Jerry observes the code of the Norwegian Bachelor Farmer: never give up, never surrender, and never change your long johns. This tends to reduce courtship to a healthy minimum, and it keeps you just as warm.

The thing to notice about a wedding ring is that it's what?... Hollow. Empty. And if you are empty too, my friend, then marriage will be a hole within a hole, and you will fall through it like a rat through an aqueduct. The only way out is when you hit bottom.

Take Your Uncle Jerry's parents. (Please.) There are 50 ways to mess up a marriage, and Your Uncle Jerry's parents have tried every single one. What keeps them together? Dental insurance. They don't want to lose their double coverage.

Point is, camper, if you can think of 5 ways out of the 50, you're a genius... and you ain't no genius. How does Uncle Jerry know? Because you're in love, duh.... Genius is a Norwegian Bachelor Farmer.

The best marriages are the practical ones. Marry for money. Marry for career advancement. Marry to get citizenship in your spouse's country. A marriage with a purpose is a marriage of true minds, young friend. Marry... to stay warm in the winter.

However, Your Uncle Jerry knows full well that few young campers will take his sage advice—the young folks WILL fall in love. And thus, for one month only, Your Uncle Jerry offers this special service.

> You can sign up for Your Uncle Jerry's Famous Online June Wedding Service. Send us your application, and Uncle Jerry will perform a no-frills, no guarantees, and no-holds-barred wedding service for you and your intended in a chat room of your choice. For the month of June only, it's free, it's convenient, and it's totally bogus. No muss, no fuss, no salesman will visit your home. (Void where prohibited by law or good sense.)

Love is in the air, camper. It's June.

Peace and joy.

CHAPTER 20
tempting fate

JUNE 14 5:05 PM

Bridget: hello good evening?

beau, r u there?

BoBoy: bridgie! hey gurl, what up?

Bridget: nothing. just felt like checking on u

BoBoy: right. in case i was up 2 something

Bridget: oh, i know ur up 2 something

BoBoy: no fair. i've been totally framed!

Bridget: i don't think so...

BoBoy: officer, please! the man was dead when i got here

Bridget: lol

BoBoy: the couch was on fire when i lay down!

Bridget: u r too funny beau boy

BoBoy: too funny 4 what?

Bridget: oh, i miss laughing. u r so good 4 me

BoBoy: awww

📨 IM from chessman

JUNE 14 5:07 PM

chessman: tatiana? hello?

tatiana? i can see you're online

Tatiana: hallo, mitchell. i am too sorry not to speak right at this moment now, you see

chessman: you can't talk now?

Tatiana: not so much, no

chessman: well, ok. i didn't want to disturb you. just checking to see how you're doing

Tatiana: no i am not doing somethings for this moment

chessman: tatiana, are you ok? you sound a little different

Tatiana: no! i am not doing somethings at this point in time, lol

chessman: um?

Tatiana: why do these american say "this point in time." lol. everyone is make fun of them. hah!

chessman: tatiana?

Tatiana: yes, my darling mitchell american boy saunders?

chessman: tatiana, have you been drinking?

Tatiana: no i have not. no no NO. yes.

chessman: i thought so

Tatiana: mitchell, i am too very sorry not to speak you now at this point in time

chessman: you're sorry?

Tatiana: no. is not how you say it. i have too much sorry. i am full of sorry. hah. i cannot recall how you very american say this. sorry?

chessman: sorrow? you're sad?

Tatiana: YES. i am SORROW. sorrow sorrow sorrow. that's the word in time. too much very sorrow to be talking american boys right now if you please thank you very much you welshman

✉ IM from Bridget

BoBoy: what do u mean u miss laughing?

Bridget: i thought that was fairly clear :)

BoBoy: are things so bad in england?

Bridget: u know the saddest thing about england?

BoBoy: what?

Bridget: no one is allowed 2 be sad

BoBoy: dude, that's no fun

Bridget: u just screw yr face up and say, fine fine i'm just fine, lovely weather we're having, stiff upper lip, what what

BoBoy: what what? i like that

Bridget: continue fine i hope it may, and yet it rained but yesterday. more tea, vicar?

BoBoy: so bridge. what's got u down in the dumps, eh? what what?

Bridget: no, that's not how u—never mind

BoBoy: u got boy trouble dontcha, bridge?

Bridget: o... u could say that. nothing that everyone hasn't been thru. quite tiresome. rather not speak of it, really

BoBoy: i knew it. come on, sweetie. what he say?

Bridget: it's what he's done, beau. it's too dreadful 4 words. i really can't. i feel myself choking up just thinking about it

BoBoy: what's he done, girlfriend?

Bridget: well, actually, it's rather simple... i believe u would say he's dumped me

BoBoy: NO

Bridget: me—of all people. i'm not that loathsome, beau, i promise u

BoBoy: what is that dude's problem??

Bridget: i've never been brilliant, but i've been told i look actually rather fetching some days

BoBoy: it's not about u, i can guarantee that

Bridget: and i AM passionate. i don't care what he says

✉ IM from chessman

chessman: tatiana, what makes you so sad? what's this about?

Tatiana: about feeling lost in my own life, mitchell. about sailing on the darkest waters

chessman: not sure i understand

Tatiana: how sad, without love, to set out across the sea

chessman: that's beautiful. it's like i've read it somewhere...

Tatiana: it is an old french poetry. oh, mitchell is there nothing you do not know?

chessman: oh, please

Tatiana: you have such a heart, my friend

chessman: i do?

Tatiana: oh my oh my. the heart of a poet. the passion of a gypsy

chessman: i'm passionate?

✉ IM from Bridget

BoBoy: of course ur, bridge. i haven't forgotten our kissing lessons, u know

Bridget: me neither :) if only...

✉ IM from chessman

Tatiana: my darling, the only way you are not the gypsy poet is that you do not read the cards

chessman: that's true. but i've seen it done

Tatiana: if only...

✉ IM from Bridget

BoBoy: if only what, bridgie?

Bridget: never mind

✉ IM from chessman

chessman: if only what, tatiana?

Tatiana: mitchell, i am too deeply sorrowed right at this moment to... but wait

chessman: what is it?

Tatiana: why have i not think of this before? you must lay the cards for me

chessman: how can i do that?

Tatiana: here. i have the cards now, and you must tell me which ones to lay down. just to give me three numbers

chessman: ok. um, 11. 29. and 47

Tatiana: all prime numbers?

chessman: sorry. i'm a nerd

Tatiana: lol. me too. ok, i count... so, and so, and so. now we see

chessman: what did we get?

Tatiana: ah, i knew. was foolish even to try. sigh

chessman: but what were the cards?

Tatiana: always the same, mitchell. 3 cards make past, present, future. so what i get is 1, 2, 3: separation, bad news, and death. always always death

chessman: i'm sorry.... johnson told me about your boyfriend

Tatiana: i turn them again, looking for love, looking for the marriage. but no: same. same. first him, then me. death. i knew it

chessman: tatiana, what do you mean?

Tatiana: so simple. fate is there to read, and one cannot change this

✎ IM from Bridget

BoBoy: come on, bridgie. let's do something 2 cheer u up

Bridget: k. tell me a story

BoBoy: a story? um, once there was a princess

Bridget: oh good

BoBoy: she lived a fairy tale life, where everything was beautiful, and she was beautiful, and she was happy all the time

Bridget: good 4 her. did she marry a prince?

BoBoy: um, well, not right away

Bridget: well, when?

BoBoy: c, first, she is captured by a dragon

Bridget: oh, exciting

BoBoy: a ferocious, obnoxticating dragon with shiny fangs, and breath that could imbue the paint off a pickup truck

Bridget: u r so funny, beau. i never knew that

BoBoy: how could u know? we just met a couple weeks ago

Bridget: who's going 2 save the princess?

BoBoy: so there's this guy. and he's out in the wilderness, cleaning his spirit. he like eats bugs and honey, barely subsiding out there

Bridget: i like how u tell a story

BoBoy: he's very sad

Bridget: why?

BoBoy: um? because his girl has left him or died or something. so he thinks that if he gets all pure in the desert... then he'll be good enough 2 rescue the princess. yeah, that's it

Bridget: pure thoughts

BoBoy: right. so he takes his vorpal sword and his silver football helmet, and he rushes off 2 fight the dragon

Bridget: the princess watches from her tower

BoBoy: the dragon blows his fiery breath, but it bounces off the silver helmet and burns him right up. then our boy chops off the dragon's head and leads the princess down from her tower

Bridget: my hero

BoBoy: happy ever after. the end

✉ IM from chessman

chessman: tatiana, maybe if i lay the cards over here?

Tatiana: how do you mean? you have the cards?

chessman: only regular cards, but they'll work, yes?

Tatiana: yes... so, you means it could be my sorrows making the cards too sad?

chessman: exactly. let's try. gimme three numbers

Tatiana: you are so lovely to do this. ok, so 7, 13, 41

chessman: prime numbers. ok, i've counted out those cards. now what?

Tatiana: so turn them and tell me

chessman: ok. first is jack of spades. what's that mean?

Tatiana: ah. so in my cards this is page of coins. well, young man. very knowledge but makes no leaping decision

chessman: not so bad, see?

Tatiana: have you the dark hair, mitchell?

chessman: i guess

Tatiana: so this could be you. surely you are the cautious one, and so brilliant <sigh>

chessman: ok ok. second card is 8 of diamonds

Tatiana: swords, of course. so very sad. alone. like the prisoner. she sigh. she weep. all around is pain to the heart. she hope it do not last forever

chessman: and that could be you, right?

Tatiana: always this is the card for me. so the last card will be some kind of death. i don't even want to know

chessman: let's see. so we have me, then you. and now... 2 of hearts?

Tatiana: NO! you are joking me?

chessman: what's it mean?

Tatiana: truly you don't know 2 of cup?

chessman: you could tell me anything and i would believe you

Tatiana: no... because you would look up

chessman: well, true...

Tatiana: you are this moment looking up the web, are you not?

chessman: busted

Tatiana: and what are you find?

chessman: 2 of cups: love, passion... union... marriage of the minds

Tatiana: lol. is it not wonderful??

chessman: um...

Tatiana: mitchell, you see? you see what this mean?

chessman: i, um...

Tatiana: is fate! is fate! you and i are the lovers. oh this make me so very happy. a new light dawns in my heart

chessman: but i don't think...

Tatiana: of course, mitchell, i know you must fight it! i know. that is so much your fate

make two more cards—any two

chessman: 7 of clubs

Tatiana: is you! you struggle. you struggle in the heart

chessman: 10 of hearts

Tatiana: i told you so. happy ever after!

✉ IM from Bridget

Bridget: beau? dance with me?

BoBoy: excuse me?

Bridget: u kissed me before. now i need 2 dance

BoBoy: but bridge, i dance like a brontosaurus

Bridget: trust me. in my mind u dance like a prince

BoBoy: oh jeeze. well, u'll have 2 teach me

Bridget: just take my right hand with yr left

BoBoy: k. got it

Bridget: now yr right hand on my waist. not too tight

BoBoy: keep my distance?

Bridget: yes, for now ;-)

my hand is on yr shoulder, and u move us to yr left, then right. again. let yr mind be quiet...

slowly 1, 2, 3, 4

BoBoy: bridget?

Bridget: mmm?

BoBoy: this is nice

Bridget: now u step back and turn 2 the left. i follow. 1, 2

BoBoy: i've never met a girl like u

Bridget: mmm... step up and turn us 2 the right

BoBoy: sometimes i get lonely. u know?

Bridget: i know, honey

BoBoy: what am i gonna do, bridge?

Bridget: turn us 1 full turn. do it in 3 steps

BoBoy: i like u so much, bridge, but i don't deserve u

Bridget: u deserve much better, my prince

BoBoy: i'm not exactly the cream of the corn

Bridget: u just need 2 believe in yrself. turn me 2 the right

BoBoy: bridget?

Bridget: yes?

BoBoy: do u believe in me?

Bridget: i do. completely

BoBoy: u don't know what that does 2 me

Bridget: everyone needs 2 feel believed in

BoBoy: u believe in yrself?

Bridget: i do when i'm with u

BoBoy: that is the nicest thing i've ever heard

Bridget: twirl me once and then catch me in yr arms

BoBoy: i was right, eh? i tromp around like a brontosaurus

Bridget: lol. u tromp divinely

≡ IM from chessman

chessman: tatiana, i don't know what to say

Tatiana: say anything. i cannot be unhappy now

chessman: this is too weird

Tatiana: yes, it is just as the gypsies tell it

chessman: but you really believe this?

Tatiana: mitchell, many thing are the mystery. shall we not believe them because we not understand?

chessman: but what are the odds of this happening?

Tatiana: the cards often have this effect

chessman: and people just believe them anyway?

Tatiana: no no. many people struggle. but what point in struggling when fate awaits us all?

chessman: i need to think

Tatiana: yes, mitchell. you think. tatiana does not rush you

chessman: will you be all right now?

Tatiana: i have not felt so well since many weeks. my heart is in the cloud

chessman: i'll write you tomorrow

Tatiana: you struggle, my page of coins. i will wait for you tomorrow

✉ IM from Bridget

BoBoy: what am i gonna do about u, bridge?

Bridget: <sigh>

BoBoy: i could just fly over there right now. i need 2 touch hands 4 real

Bridget: what if there's a dragon?

BoBoy: got my helmet right here

Bridget: come 4 me, soon, beau. i'm here in my tower

CHAPTER 21
china wall

✉ IM from gothling

JUNE 15 10:50 PM

gothling: so, johnson, are we good 2 go?

alfonso: almost set

gothling: perfect. my gurls got them right 2 the brink last night

alfonso: so the gypsy stuff?

gothling: worked like a charm

alfonso: great. k. well. cya

gothling: hey!

alfonso: yes?

gothling: that's it? the brush off?

alfonso: not really. why?

gothling: where's the good ol johnson? where's the banter? the flirtation?

alfonso: u made things pretty clear on that the last time

gothling: so what's yr point? u get 2 freeze me out because i said no?

alfonso: i'm not freezing u out. but i do have feelings 2 protect, just like u

gothling: get over it, dude. ur still mine—admit it

alfonso: i don't think so, annie

gothling: come on, johnson. ur not hurt. yr ego's bruised is all

alfonso: are we done?

gothling: k, look. i'm sorry. i'm sorry i was... i'm sorry if whatever i said caused a problem. let's just let it go and get back 2 the way things were

alfonso: well, thanks 4 the apology, but I forgave u b4

gothling: o, thank u so much, u patronizing putz. then why r u being cold now?

alfonso: sorry, i don't mean 2 be cold

gothling: all right, then

alfonso: but if u think nothing's changed, ur wrong

gothling: johnson, u may not behave this way. GROW. UP.

alfonso: grown up means consequences, annie.
i'm not mad. but after u dis a person enough times,
they tend 2 protect themselves

gothling: get real. u still need me and u know it

alfonso: seriously, g2g. i'll keep u posted about the
chat room

gothling: whatever, dude

EXCHANGE STUDENT ROOM **UNION HIGH SCHOOL**

JUNE 15 11:00 PM

BoBoy has entered

BoBoy:	yo y'all. anybody alive yet?
alfonso:	bro beau! what ease thee word?
BoBoy:	word, J. good 2 c ur still the wittiest of them all
alfonso:	my new accent. jamaican. whaddya think?
BoBoy:	kewl. why u doing that?
alfonso:	jus messin. i like tatiana's talk is all
BoBoy:	yeah, but that's her real accent
alfonso:	well, what's real online?
BoBoy:	meaning what—she's faking? i don't theeenk so
alfonso:	i just mean a lot of people wear masks
BoBoy:	masks. dude, u have a seriously cold view of human beings

Bridget has entered

Bridget: hello, good evening. am i the first?

alfonso: no indeed, bridget. beau and i r here

BoBoy: **hey gurl. what up?**

Bridget: ah, my prince! i did so hope u would come 2nite

alfonso: prince?? dude, what have i missed?

BoBoy: **oh, heh heh. i was um, telling fairy tales last
                 night. dragons, princes, u know. swords**

alfonso: oic. bridget, u be careful. the stories our
                boy can tell...

Bridget: lol. not 2 worry. i know a tall tale when i hear it

Tatiana has entered

alfonso: hallo, tatiana, my velly good fren

Tatiana: what is happen to the johnson voice?

BoBoy: **tatiana, pay no attention 2 the man behind
                 the jamaican t-shirt**

Bridget: that was a shock, rather, i should say

chessman has entered

chessman: made it

BoBoy: **zup, bro?**

Bridget: hello, good morning

chessman: hi, bridget

Bridget: or evening, rather. i'm always confused. how tiresome

alfonso: mitchell, my good mon. welcome 2
                da cabana

chessman: johnson?

Tatiana: something very troubling is happen to johnson. he seem to think he is of jamaica this evening. has the t-shirt and all

alfonso: nutting could be furder from da troot. i only showin me boy how de life online be whatevah we want

BoBoy: or something like that

alfonso: more rum, my brotha?

✉ IM from Bridget

Bridget: beau, i'm sorry about calling u my prince. did i embarrass u?

BoBoy: nah

Bridget: i was just so pleased 2 see u

BoBoy: 's all right

Bridget: ur still my prince, tho :)

BoBoy: that sounds so funny. but nice...

✉ IM from Tatiana

Tatiana: mitchell, please tell me what is problem with johnson?

chessman: not sure i know. he's not stupid, so i think he must have a point to make

Tatiana: is very—how you say?—irritable?

chessman: ah. irritating

Tatiana: very irritating to me

chessman: maybe he'll stop in a minute. i'm sure he isn't mocking you

EXCHANGE STUDENT ROOM **UNION HIGH SCHOOL**

Bridget: johnson, do the voice again

alfonso: which voice do that be, me ladee?

Bridget: that's the 1. very funny

chessman: just a side note, johnson.
              we still have that agreement?

alfonso: yah mon, deed we doo

chessman: so then, if one of the exchange students
              found the voice irritating, you would
              probably cut it out. am i right?

alfonso: ahem, well, yes that would seem 2 be in the spirit
              of the agreement

Tatiana: so you are your real voice again, johnson?
              thank you for this

alfonso: my real mask, yes, my queen

BoBoy: **johnson's not telling us something**

Bridget: lol. many things, no doubt

BoBoy: **no, i mean he usually yanks chain when he's
              not happy**

chessman: dude, that's right. i never put
              it together like that

alfonso: thank u 4 yr concern, bubba, but the j-man
              is totally fine. not a cloud in the sky, not a care
              in the world

chessman: oh, there's a problem

Tatiana: lol. you mean he has perhap the woman
              trouble, yes?

alfonso: as if. okay, group, let's talk about
----->school

chessman: let's talk about compassion, dude

alfonso: don't go there, nerdman. we'll all be sorry

BoBoy: mitchie, u dawg. u done nailed it

✉ IM from Tatiana

Tatiana: mitchell, i am so happy from last night, i want only to be with you. is that rude to others?

chessman: no, you're fine

Tatiana: and have you struggled with 2 of hearts?

chessman: tatiana, this is so difficult for me.
i would never do anything to hurt my girlfriend, but...

Tatiana: i know is true. is true. but she have been away for so very long time, yes?

chessman: she has

Tatiana: how are you sure she isn't telling you goodbye?

chessman: <sigh> that's what i'm afraid of

EXCHANGE STUDENT ROOM **UNION HIGH SCHOOL**

Bridget: talk about compassion 4 who? what r u chaps saying?

BoBoy: **johnson, be honest. ur among friends**

alfonso: never

chessman: bro, i think you can trust these women

BoBoy: **group hug for johnson!! {{j-man}}**

Tatiana: yes, please. we can be trusted in matters of love

alfonso: ur making a big deal out of nothing

BoBoy: **aha**

alfonso: a small disaster of the heart. nothing a young poet can't endure alone

BoBoy: **aw man. she didn't!**

Bridget: can this be true? johnson has a heart? ;-)

chessman: his heart is at a delicate stage right now. he's gone cold turkey. he's opened up to the one he's wanted all along

alfonso: no names, guys, or u WILL be sorry

BoBoy: **dude, we got yr back**

Bridget: i'm so embarrassed. johnson, i had no idea

Tatiana: please to forgive bridget. it was teasing only

alfonso: oh, u people... just drop it k? i can deal with a little rejection

BoBoy: **she did! she crushed him**

chessman: crushed? never. only a flesh
wound, right J? we're here for you

alfonso: mitch, ur a funny guy. u never liked me,
anyway

✉ IM from Bridget

Bridget: beau, what in the world??

BoBoy: it's real. i can tell he's been dissed

Bridget: i'm so sorry. who would have done it?

BoBoy: can't tell u that, sweetie. but it's almost never
happened before

EXCHANGE STUDENT ROOM **UNION HIGH SCHOOL**

chessman: dude, i'm a loyal pooch. how many
friends do you think i have?

alfonso: more than me

Tatiana: johnson, i tell you this in all seriously.
a wound of the heart is need the air to heal.
know what i meaning? not matters
how small

alfonso: will u puhleeze give it a rest?

BoBoy: **big breaths, J**

chessman: you want i should wipe her hard
drive, boss?

alfonso: lol

Tatiana: beau boy, you know these girl who have hurt the johnson?

BoBoy: oh, dude, we know her, all right. she's a cruel 1

chessman: dawg, johnson likes her. therefore, we like her

Bridget: how can u like her after this?

BoBoy: zackly

chessman: compassion where due. haven't you been paying attention?

BoBoy: oh, right. true. she's had it rough. well, but still...

alfonso: pleeze pleeze pleeze pleeze pleeze

✉ IM from Tatiana

chessman: tatiana, we need to talk about us, and here's the thing that i can't get beyond. if i would leave my girl to fall in love with you...

Tatiana: ah, mitchell, i love it so when you say these word

chessman: if i would leave HER, how could YOU ever trust me?

Tatiana: no, you would never do to me. i know this

chessman: no you don't

Tatiana: because i would never leave you for months without any word

chessman: you CAN'T know this. don't you see?

Tatiana: no. don't you see, mitchell? is fate in the cards

chessman: aw, man...

Tatiana: you think that is nothing?

chessman: not exactly, but still

Tatiana: destiny is not to be played with. the cards say we are marriage in future, and this is all i need to know

---

EXCHANGE STUDENT ROOM **UNION HIGH SCHOOL**

alfonso: ok, u broke me down. here's the story

Bridget: good. i love stories

alfonso: ok, yes. YES, so i had this big crush going 4 a certain person. but i knew she was closed up. she's a castle. she's the china wall. she lets no 1 in

BoBoy: **she's a brick**

alfonso: why i thought i could get thru, of all people, i'll never know

chessman: because you're good at it?

alfonso: but i decided 2 go with hope instead of fear: i told her how i felt

Tatiana: you are the brave man, johnson. total respect, you dude

alfonso: i laid my heart at her feet, and she stomped that sucker flat

Bridget: that's terrible!

BoBoy: **dude, i'll flatten her tires**

alfonso: no no no. that's the point. i can take it. i'm not complaining. i knew what i was risking, and i will accept this hurt from her

chessman: oh, he's got it bad

alfonso: she is, after all, magnificent

Tatiana: very poetic

Bridget: it's so sweet. i'm actually crying here

alfonso: but i will not try again

Tatiana: oh no, absolutely you must try again!

Bridget: of course u will. don't even think u won't

alfonso: WHAAA???

chessman: they're saying you gotta try again, bro

Bridget: no, u must! or else u didn't mean it the first time

alfonso: u people r barking mad

BoBoy: **dude, they're right**

alfonso: r u not listening??

Bridget: what kind of a poet would bail?

Tatiana: do you love these woman or not?

alfonso: u hate me. u just want 2 see me flattened again

Bridget: if u luv her, u keep trying

Tatiana: is simple, really

Bridget: u don't know what flat is

alfonso: excuse me?? is that some kinda english joke?

Bridget: u don't. watching her walk away with someone else— that would be flat

Tatiana: losing her to your best friend

alfonso: arrrgh. that is such a cruel card 2 play

BoBoy: bro, u see why i like these girls?

alfonso: people skills?

BoBoy: all their passion, dude

✉ IM from Bridget

Bridget: oh u big sweetie!

BoBoy: what i say?

Bridget: ur so good 2 me. how come u can c what... u know... that english dude can't?

BoBoy: don't worry about the past, peanut

Bridget: u mean it?

BoBoy: i mean it

Bridget: tell me

BoBoy: i've got it bad 4 u, girl. from here on out, it's u and me. i swear it is

Bridget: ah, beau. this is too sweet. and too sad

BoBoy: take my hand

Bridget: got it, guy

BoBoy: why too sad?

Bridget: oh just everything. i'll tell u l8r

alfonso: ok. \<huff puff huff puff\> supposing i really was loser enough 2 go back and try again. what would be my best approach? just hypothetically

Tatiana: well...

Bridget: best case scenario: she didn't mean it

alfonso: didn't mean it...

Tatiana: oh, johnson, please. you know about this

Bridget: she could be buying time 2 think

chessman: she WHAT??? can they DO that??

alfonso: well... yeah, they can. i just didn't think...

Tatiana: so did you part in anger?

alfonso: not at all. she IM'd today

Bridget: good, and how did u act toward her?

alfonso: um...

BoBoy: u said "i don't need no scumbag love," right?

chessman: right: contumelious

BoBoy: dude, is that what that means?

chessman: looked it up

alfonso: i was polite but... let's say distant

Tatiana: excellent, johnson.

Bridget: cool but not cold, right?

alfonso: i guess

Bridget: is he a natural or what?

Tatiana: and she not like this, correct?

alfonso: not really

Bridget: ok, so keep it that way 4 next time

Tatiana: so she know you mean it, but not so
               she give up the hope

BoBoy: **man, this is brutal**

alfonso: no, i get it. these guys r very good

Tatiana: she is always asking for gravel, yes?

alfonso: say what?

chessman: making you grovel

alfonso: oh that. yes, indeed. very much the alpha dog
               personality

Tatiana: so you not make the grovel ever more.
               understood me? ever

Bridget: that DOESN'T mean be a total jerk

Tatiana: meeting as equals, very important

chessman: how about flowers, candy?

Bridget: oh quite. but in good time. when she earns them

BoBoy: **when she earns them! dang, that's cool. i can
               never think of that stuff**

Tatiana: send a poetry, perhaps

BoBoy: **all in good time**

Bridget: and poetry doesn't have 2 be gravelly, u know

alfonso: of course. it can be angry, mocking, despairing,
               kind... still, i don't think this is going anywhere.
               she's quite firm

chessman: should you read his cards, tatiana?

Tatiana: of course. one moment

alfonso: now this stuff, i don't totally buy

Tatiana: the cards do not care if you buy them, my friend. your fate, still your fate is. ready?

BoBoy: **ready. what do they say?**

Tatiana: give to me 3 numbers, johnson

alfonso: 14, 23, 27, hut hut

Tatiana: good. thank you

chessman: so she counts off your 3 cards, bro

Tatiana: first one turning. ah, queen of sword. strong but troubled. is true? she broods, she lets few near. waves her heartbreak like a sword

BoBoy: **bingo**

alfonso: are u doing this 4 real?

chessman: she is, dude

alfonso: tatiana, really? i didn't know u knew this stuff

chessman: learned it from the gypsies

alfonso: why do i suddenly feel like someone's pulling my strings?

Tatiana: second card is page of sword. hmm... sword and sword

BoBoy: **what's the page mean?**

Tatiana: is johnson. intelligent. wishes to be good person, but perhaps a spy.... johnson keeps a secret

alfonso: lol. not me

chessman: oh, never any secrets

BoBoy: **his heart is an open file**

Tatiana: both are swords. so very difficult relationship, yes? always the dueling

alfonso: k, tatiana. i don't get this. u really don't know me that well

Tatiana: i know you only from these chat room, as you can witness

alfonso: so how r u doing this?

BoBoy: **dude it's the cards. she's just reading them**

alfonso: get real

Tatiana: mr. johnson, do i know you? do i know this girl of whom you love?

alfonso: no, i get ya. how could someone in albania know her?

BoBoy: **k then. what's the next card?**

alfonso: mitch, r u buying this?

chessman: there's lots of fate in opera, dude. i'm surprised you're not eating it up

alfonso: opera is different. this here is like reading my mail

Tatiana: next card? or put them away?

alfonso: ok, but against my better judgment

Tatiana: turning... how strange

Bridget: what?

Tatiana: how very strange

alfonso: oh, she's playing with me now

BoBoy: **tatiana, u got us all worried over here**

Tatiana: so sorry. it is... major death card

Bridget: death??

alfonso: yipes! not me, i hope?

Tatiana: no you don't understand. there are
            many death cards

BoBoy: dude, ur fish food now. road kill city. ur toast

chessman: what does it mean, tatiana?

Tatiana: this one is not death like you die,
            johnson. death like you change

alfonso: huh?

Tatiana: out with old, in with new

Bridget: oh, i get it

chessman: wow, like reincarnation?

Tatiana: or resurrection. is change...

alfonso: makes no sense

BoBoy: check it out, dawg, it's change—yr new leaf!

alfonso: my new leaf!

✉ IM from Tatiana

chessman: tatiana, you are amazing

Tatiana: really, my handsome american boy? why you
say this?

chessman: what you're doing for johnson

Tatiana: but i am do nothing

chessman: giving him new hope. i can't tell you how much that means to him

Tatiana: you misunderstand, mitchell. i reading cards only

chessman: you're not pulling the cards to make him feel better?

Tatiana: you mean am i cheating?

chessman: you might be "helping"

Tatiana: did you help when you laid 2 of hearts for us?

chessman: i wouldn't know how

Tatiana: i never help either

chessman: i love you even more for that

Tatiana: i know you do

chessman: wait. did i just say that?

Tatiana: you did. I am smiling

EXCHANGE STUDENT ROOM **UNION HIGH SCHOOL**

Bridget: but what about the girl? what happens with her?

Tatiana: i do not know. it would take another card

chessman: johnson?

alfonso: not me

BoBoy: **what??? u don't want 2 know?**

alfonso: no way

Bridget: o i hate this. ack ack, i can't stand not knowing

alfonso: don't press my luck, gurl

chessman: maybe 3 cards is enough

alfonso: it's enough 4 me

BoBoy: **maybe like a new leaf 4 both? how bout that?**

Tatiana: could be

alfonso: or not. doesn't matter

Bridget: arrrgh. i want that caaarrrrrrrrrddd :-(

alfonso: i'd rather be surprised. i really would

chessman: well done, J

alfonso: besides, i just had a thought. gotta run

Tatiana: you see, mr. johnson. you have many weapons in the battle for her heart

BoBoy: **scale the wall, baby**

Bridget: gotta run? why?

chessman: going to start a poem?

alfonso has left the room

BoBoy: **bingo**

CHAPTER 22
calling jerry

JUNE 16 8:00 PM

alfonso: yo annie

gothling: u gotta be kidding. i thought u weren't speaking 2 me

alfonso: come on. i never said that. we've got business 2 do

gothling: what business?

alfonso: the girls didn't talk 2 u?

gothling: haven't heard from them. OR from u

alfonso: ok, well, here's what u need 2 know. the dudes have walked into the trap. it's time 2 spring it

gothling: well, finally. and were u ever going 2 tell me? u said u'd keep me posted

alfonso: will u stop? so we just need some evidence for the real bliss and ms. T 2 find. something the dudes can't deny

gothling: johnson, i KNOW. i know all this

alfonso: yes. fine

gothling: i know EXACTLY what the next step is! i'm the one who thought this whole game UP!!

alfonso: chill, annie

gothling: don't u "chill" me! I'M the one who brought u in, u troll. u insect. u troglodyte!

alfonso: look, i don't have even a minute 4 a shouting match

gothling: I AM NOT SHOUTING!!

alfonso: k. so what i was thinking was this

gothling: JOHNSON!!!

alfonso: hush, annabelle. y'll hurt yrself

gothling: johnson?

alfonso: yes?

gothling: i hate u

alfonso: i know. now can we move on?

gothling: seriously. i loathe u. i really do

alfonso: i think we need uncle jerry

gothling: what?

alfonso: u got him that online minister degree, didn't u?

gothling: oh arrrgh. i see where ur going with this....

alfonso: u don't like it?

gothling: no, i HATE it. it's much better than my idea

alfonso: oic. well, we can call it yr idea. no problem

gothling: DON'T PATRONIZE ME. I HATE THAT!!

alfonso: u hate so many things today

gothling: only everything about u

alfonso: so do we have a deal?

gothling: YES. now shove off

The Big Reveal
16 JUNE

> *The Road of Excess leads
> to the Palace of Wisdom.*
> *—Wm Blake, lame old proverb*

Joy and peace, camper. Your wise old Uncle Jerry has found that there comes a time in every camper's life when all must be revealed. These are the moments— sometimes painful—from which we learn, and through which we may enter... (wait for it...) the gates of wisdom!

As you would know, young person, if you had been reading Your Uncle Jerry's Sunday Sermons like you oughta (get them in PDF at a website near you), most campers hike the Road of Excess without a clue.

Now. What is the Road of Excess? Anyone? Oh dear, oh dear. The Road, the Way—listen at me—the very Life we lead is a journey paved in disappointments and desires. Young people wish for so much as they travel life's pathway, do they not? And are not their little boats so often dashed upon the rocks and reefs of despair?

Ah well, Your Uncle Jerry was young once too.

Onward we slog, knee-deep in illusions, clouded by hopes. "She loves me." "He needs me." "There will never be another." "Something deep inside cannot be denied."

How long we must travel thus, we never know. But one day we turn a corner, the clouds part, the light breaks. And... voila!... all is REVEALED. Like dawn at the landfill.

(A poet friend gave Your Uncle Jerry that line. Can a poet be a true friend? you ask. Excellent. The question shows you have been studying. Your Uncle Jerry is not sure. A poet could be friend or foe. Beware. Treat a poet with excess of caution.)

Where were we? Excess. Ah yes. (A rhyme! Perhaps Your Uncle Jerry is a poet. Hah! I jokes.)

Your Uncle Jerry knows four young campers traveling the Road of Excess even as we speak. Tonight will be the night when Your Uncle Jerry will part the foolish clouds of romance that shroud their minds and show these hapless campers into the clean well-lighted Palace of Wisdom.

Peace and joy.

CHAPTER 23
entr@pment

GURLGANG ROOM
JUNE 16 10:50 PM

bliss4u:	oh, i am so mad at him
gothling:	**told u. did i not tell u?**
Ms.T:	u did tell us
bliss4u:	i'm just going 2 kill him. mitchie, how could u do this 2 me?
Ms.T:	i know, bliss. i know
gothling:	**u trusted him. that was yr mistake**
Ms.T:	on the upside, he held out for a long time...
bliss4u:	don't make excuses 4 him. he's toast. i thought he was strong but he's a slut puppy
gothling:	**just like the rest of them**

Ms.T:	yeah, miss bridget. you took beau down in seconds
bliss4u:	beau's got a kind heart. that's his only failing
Ms.T:	i can think of a few others, which i intend to describe to him in detail
bliss4u:	ur not really mad r u?
Ms.T:	i could spit nails
bliss4u:	pretty quiet about it
Ms.T:	if i talk about it i just start to cry
bliss4u:	start? i cried all night. now i'm pissed
Ms.T:	not me. i need to hold this edge or i'll go all mushy
gothling:	**u people. what a pair of wusses**
Ms.T:	you know, annie, i could displace some of my fury in your direction
gothling:	**why me? i did nothing**
bliss4u:	u set us up, as i recall...
Ms.T:	i didn't say you DESERVED it. i just said i could DO it
gothling:	**grow up. u lost a bet, that's all**
bliss4u:	i lost mitchie. that's what i lost
gothling:	**love's a gamble, gurl. u knew that going in**
Ms.T:	u can't really be that cold, can you annie?
gothling:	**i'm just not sentimental. this stuff happens 2 the best of us**

alfonso has entered

alfonso:	ladies, u ready 2 go?
bliss4u:	can't we just skip this part?
gothling:	**no way no way no way**
Ms.T:	and that's because...?
alfonso:	listen, i know u feel like this is a disaster
bliss4u:	that would be 1 way 2 put it
alfonso:	but if u quit now, the dudes will never see what they've done
bliss4u:	but why NOT? it's perfectly obvious
alfonso:	not 2 them it isn't
Ms.T:	what are you saying, johnson?
bliss4u:	r they that stupid?
alfonso:	no, look. they've only put a toe in the shallow stuff. they need 2 cross the river
gothling:	**i just hate how well u say things sometimes**
Ms.T:	i think i get it
alfonso:	this is the last bit we do
gothling:	**their eyes will be opened**
alfonso:	and they will c
gothling:	**so please, ladies. masks up 1 last time**
Ms.T:	och, this old mask. something is smell about it
alfonso:	lol, tatiana
bliss4u:	i'm so mad
alfonso:	...and into the chat room, please

EXCHANGE STUDENT ROOM **UNION HIGH SCHOOL**

JUNE 16 11:00 PM

Tatiana has entered

Bridget has entered

alfonso: tatiana! bridget! u made it

BoBoy: hey, bridge. i thought u were going 2 stand me up this time

Bridget: u americans r so impatient

Tatiana: precisely, i would have think a beautiful women is worth the waiting

chessman: i couldn't agree more, tatiana

Tatiana: there, you see beau? mitchell knows how to wait for a lady

Bridget: i suppose mitchell thinks some women r worth waiting 4 and some aren't, what what?

alfonso: ok, great. here's the thing

BoBoy: yeah but how can a guy be sure how long 2 wait? maybe she's not coming

Tatiana: trust! is that how you say in english? loving means believing! may i call you BeauZeau?

alfonso: k, this is going 2 be a terrific end 2 the summer chat room. i was thinking we could talk about relationship customs in different countries

BoBoy: yikes! dude, what i say?

Bridget: nothing, sweetie. ur fine

chessman: tatiana, is everything ok?

Bridget: she'll be fine. under a little stress lately, u know?

Tatiana: mitchell, you must pardon my directness

alfonso: customs? different countries? anyone?

chessman: of course, tatiana. what's up?

Tatiana: you must marry me

chessman: excuse me?

BoBoy: **whoa, dude. that's direct all right**

Tatiana: it is only for online. you know, the online
             marriage

chessman: i'm not sure i understand

Tatiana: you will not see me till the september,
             but i must know that you are mine
             until then

chessman: can we talk about this on the side?

Bridget: no, let's all do it! what a loverly idea. wouldn't that
             be loverly?

BoBoy: **what? like u and me, bridge?**

Bridget: how exciting. i can imagine u in tuxedo, my big footballer.
             woof!

Tatiana: johnson can arrange it, i having no doubt

alfonso: an online wedding? if that's what the ladies
             wish, i can c what's possible

BoBoy: **k, time-out, kids! ur scaring me here**

chessman: tatiana, i'm not sure why it's so
             important all of a sudden

Bridget: oh, dear. we're scaring the american boys... hee hee

Tatiana: yes, well, my darling mitchell. i think
             about how you spoke of trusting. i need
             to trust that you will wait for me

Bridget: pleeeze, beau? it's only a game. it'll be fun. besides, it's just online...

BoBoy: **well, true**

Bridget: everyone's doing it in england. then they get divorced the next day. how fun!

chessman: can you take it that lightly?

BoBoy: **i haven't technically broken up with ms. T yet**

Tatiana: yes, well, is she not gone forever?

chessman: we don't know... that's what is so weird

BoBoy: **they like disappeared in a very fishy way**

alfonso: actually, i... um, i'm thinking things have changed 4 them

chessman: ok. what have you heard J?

alfonso: well, i didn't mean 2 bring it up in a large group, but i did hear something

BoBoy: **don't tell me they called annie again**

alfonso: ah, well, it seems they did

chessman: so is there a message, or are you just tooling us here?

alfonso: so... well, she says they actually didn't mention you. i'm not sure what this means

Bridget: oh not good

alfonso: bliss's grandmother is much better, so they could come back if they wanted 2. but... well, they've decided 2 stay awhile

BoBoy: **what?? why??**

Tatiana: women have their reasons, my friend

BoBoy: **there's someone else, isn't there?**

alfonso: i don't think it's official, no

chessman: johnson, this isn't going to work. spill it... whatever you got

alfonso: k. <ahem> annie says they talked about 2 guys they met... 2 guys who r a lot of fun. evidently, it's hard 2 say goodbye

BoBoy: **i knew it**

chessman: so they're not even going to tell us it's over?

alfonso: hold on, don't jump 2 conclusions. i don't believe they've decided it's over. that may depend on u

BoBoy: **come on, bro. how bogus is that? they're the ones who left**

alfonso: look, dawg. they're girls at 16. they're alive. they have needs. maybe they've made a mistake, maybe not. the heart... is unruly

chessman: i don't know where that leaves us

alfonso: well, i'm not 1 to give advice, but... u gotta ask yrself 2 things. 1: if the worst has happened, can u move on? obviously u can

Bridget: oh, excuse me. i thought we had moved on already. beau?

chessman: what's the second thing?

alfonso: 2. if she comes back, can u forgive and not ask too many questions?

Tatiana: johnson seem to have the experience in these matter...

BoBoy: **not ask about the other dudes?... hmm**

alfonso: well, 1 thing is sure. <cough cough> no 1 here is in a position 2 criticize

chessman: true enough. i'm not pointing fingers

Tatiana: and where are the BeauZeau fingers pointing?

BoBoy: no, in a way... i'm actually relieved

Tatiana: relieved?

BoBoy: totally, like the pressure is off, now

Tatiana: you'll not speak to this girl T, first?

chessman: tatiana, we've tried. if she wanted to talk, she's had plenty of chances

BoBoy: seems like she wants 2 talk 2 other people

Bridget: u do like me, don't u, beau? ur not just missing her? because i need 2 know now

BoBoy: bridget...

Bridget: u talked me down from that ledge, and i'm so weary of being sad

Tatiana: mitchell, you said if you could leave your girl, how could i trust you wouldn't do this same thing to me.

chessman: yes, i said that

Tatiana: so, it seems you don't have a girl now. but i have found the way to trust. you must marry to me, eh? only online, not forever. only to save you for me till i get there.

Bridget: oh yes, let's do it. we all need a laugh

BoBoy: boy that's the truth

chessman: i need a minute to think

Bridget: beau, sweetie. take my hand. i'm leaning out over the water, and it is so very very far 2 fall...

Tatiana: i know is a soon thing, but mitchell, i am such
            the desperate woman without knowing i can
            trust

chessman: you can trust me. you can trust the cards

BoBoy: **bridget, i'm reaching out... and now i'm... tickling
            u in the ribs!**

Bridget: lol

Tatiana: sometime the cards do not telling, but rather
            making the question: so, 2 of hearts—he
            loves me! or he loves me?
            oh, sorry: is the talk of love too much
            for the genius american?

chessman: tatiana, what can i say? i crossed that
            bridge the other night. truly i did

Tatiana: see, darling mitchell? your passion runs deep
            and simple. you could be albanian!

chessman: funny

Tatiana: so will you "marry" me and put my fears
            to rest?

Bridget: yes yes. johnson, run get us a priest or something

alfonso: **i'm on it. back in a flash with the preacher man**

chessman: tatiana, ok. if you need this to be
            sure of me till september, then ok

 TXT to gothling

June 16 11:16 pm

From: Johnson

rdy whn u r

Bridget: then ur still my prince?

BoBoy: **i am**

Bridget: take me down the aisle?

BoBoy: **u bet**

 TXT to Johnson

June 16 11:17 pm
From: gothling
m on it

alfonso: dudes and dudettes, i'm back and i've got
             what we need. this will go down in chat
             room history

JerryC has entered

alfonso: Jerry! welcome. meet tatiana, meet bridget,
             meet mitch and beau

JerryC: **GREETINGS! joy and peace, peace
             and joy**

alfonso: group, this is Jerry Clarkson, scout leader,
             netizen, and minister of the online word

JerryC: you can call me J or you can call me C. but just don't call me JC, heh heh heh. he's in a cyber space all his own ;) ;)

chessman: oh my oh my oh my

Tatiana: welcome jerry. and we are understanding that you make the marriage online?

Bridget: he's so friendly, isn't he, beau?

BoBoy: way friendly

JerryC: indeed i do, miss tatiana, indeed i doobie doobie doo. i can marry and bury, chastise, baptize, dry clean, and treat a young man's frostbite of the toes, all at 100 megabits per second. heh heh heh

Tatiana: is wonderful. just what is needed

JerryC: sign up for my weekly e-sermons, young man, delivering peace and joy in pdf every saturday midnight—while ur out doing what you shouldn't oughta ;-) ;-) that's a joke, son.

alfonso: excellent, J. we won't keep u long. we just need a quick online double wedding

BoBoy: mitch, can this be real?

chessman: i guess so. anyone can get a license to do this

BoBoy: but is the marriage real, then?

Bridget: oh look, my fiancé has frostbite already :)

Tatiana: a disaster

JerryC: may i just say this, my brothers...

alfonso: and sisters

JerryC: and sisters, tx alfonso

alfonso: no problem

JerryC: ladies...

alfonso: and gentlemen

JerryC: dearly beloved, marriage is what brings us 2gether. peace and joy

alfonso: say it preacher

JerryC: life online is as real as you make it. i have known many and many a happy young couple that got hitched right here at the altar of the ethernet

alfonso: joy and peace

JerryC: thank you brother

alfonso: or sister

JerryC: or sis... ok, stow it, johnson. i'll take it from here

alfonso: tell it, jerry

chessman: wait a minute

JerryC: many a happy man and woman making it real, many a boy and girl making it last, and they—like you—started right here in the great bright temple of the net, right here in the solemn presence of the all-seeing web

alfonso: that's just beautiful

chessman: johnson, this guy knows you?

JerryC: peace and joy. and here in the presence of that awesome cyberosity, we gather 2nite 2 draw these 2 young couples near. and 2 bind them, if you will, with the very tie that bindeth all humanity. all for 1, and 1 for all, and likewise even unto the other (alfonso can you play a sound file right here?)

alfonso: no can do, rev. let's move along

JerryC: joy and peace, where was i? will the unwitting subjects—i mean the loving couples heh heh heh—please join me down front here. blessings, blessings on u. and when i ask u a question, son, u speak right up in the microphone. i joke. heh heh. i joke because i luv

Bridget: oh, i'm excited. thank u beau. thank u for being such a dear. u can say it's only online if u want, but 2 me it's everything

BoBoy: i know, hon

Bridget: it's all i've got

chessman: tatiana, i have to say i'm a little nervous here

Tatiana: is fine, my handsome american boy. this jerry fellow very nice, like russian priest i think

BoBoy: i think he's been hitting the sacred vodka 2nite

JerryC: 2 quick questions, boys, and life will never be the same: will you take these 2 flowers of the forest, dew-picked in the early sweetness of their bloom, 2 be your wedded online brides? answer prompt and don't mumble ;) :) :D

BoBoy: yessir i will

chessman: yes

alfonso: oh, i told myself i wasn't going 2 cry....

JerryC: and ladies, will you accept these strapping, handsome, though none 2 bright young units 2 be yr wedded online grooms, constantly at yr beck and call, falling over their feet 2 apologize and do yr bidding? now's the time 2 back out if yr hands ain't tied. do ya want em or dontcha?

Bridget: i do i do i do

Tatiana: yes, i... oh mitchell, yes i do

alfonso: i knew it. there goes the mascara...

JerryC: is there anyone here who knows a reason why (scuse me while i dab my eyes)

alfonso: oh, me too. me too

JerryC: is there anyone here who knows why these 4 loving morons should NOT be joined in wondrous online matrimony?

alfonso: not a 1, rev. many thanks

JerryC: my work is done

JerryC has left the room

Bridget has left the room

Tatiana has left the room

BoBoy: hey, where'd they go?

alfonso: don't worry, handsome. they'll be back in a flash

chessman: johnson, where'd you come up with Uncle Jerry?

bliss4u has entered

Ms.T has entered

BoBoy: hey, stranger!

chessman: bliss??

BoBoy: wait a sec. what r u doing here??

bliss4u: mitchie, why why why why?

BoBoy: **oh dawg, we r totally imbued**

alfonso: truer words were never spoken

chessman: wait... i'm still...

Ms.T: still what, mitchell darling?

alfonso: come on, bro. it's not that hard 2 work out

gothling has entered

chessman: i was afraid you'd say that. this whole foreign student thing was...

alfonso: bogosity, dude

gothling: **maskosity**

BoBoy: **annie's here too?**

gothling: **i was in the area. thought i'd...**

bliss4u: pop round, what what

BoBoy: **T, i'm innocent. those girls totally played us**

Ms.T: don't even. you had your eyes wide open

chessman: i'm getting it now. annie, you're Jerry C, aren't you?

gothling: **peace and joy, dude**

BoBoy: **excuse me?**

chessman: bro—annie and johnson burned us bad

bliss4u: oh, like ur the 1 who got burned? u married my best friend right behind my back

chessman: true. and you've been lying since the story about your grandmother

gothling: **an innocent fiction**

BoBoy: **bliss? yr best friend is tatiana?**

Ms.T: BEAU! wake up! i was tatiana!

alfonso:	and wasn't she wonderful? what a performance
chessman:	shut up, johnson
Ms.T:	how kind you americans are, darling
BoBoy:	**i'm starting 2 get it, now**
alfonso:	and bliss was just brilliant as bridget
bliss4u:	thank u, johnson. we had brilliant coaches
chessman:	bliss. tamra. did you think this was funny? did we deserve this? do you not have lives?
bliss4u:	u can't blame us. u went 4 these chicks of yr own free will
BoBoy:	**what free will? u totally lied 2 us**
gothling:	**sweet sweet sweet**
chessman:	shut up, annie
Ms.T:	nobody dragged you down the aisle, bubba
chessman:	no, they hinted about suicide
alfonso:	true. and i warned them that was over the top
BoBoy:	**shut up, johnson**
gothling:	**there's no way 2 spin this, my dawgs. u done the deed**
chessman:	you can't be serious
bliss4u:	we were there, mitchie. we saw u
chessman:	no, bliss. "you" weren't there. i'm not even sure who "you" are
alfonso:	**ur caught, bro. a classic setup**
chessman:	more like classic entrapment. and are we supposed to trust that this is the real bliss and tam now?

BoBoy: T, come on, how can u blame us, when u were totally tooling us?

Ms.T: i can blame you because you promised you'd be good

BoBoy: oh, and like U were good? didn't u hit on my man mitch?

Ms.T: that wasn't real, and you know it

chessman: then what WE said wasn't real, either. nothing about this was real

bliss4u: it was too, mitch. i could tell u meant it

BoBoy: gurl, how could u tell? u were somebody else

bliss4u: i don't even know what that means

✉ IM from chessman

chessman: tamra, what's real?

Ms.T: what do you mean?

chessman: are you real or was tatiana?

Ms.T: tatiana who?

chessman: no more games, T. this whole thing was beneath you

Ms.T: ask me a real question and i'll tell you

chessman: ok. my real question is did you have real feelings for the real me or not?

Ms.T: mitchell, i can't go there. you know i can't

chessman: you CAN go there. i'm not asking you to leave beau. i'm only saying i'm not a toy, and I'm not ashamed of what i felt for you

Ms.T: felt?

chessman: ok... feel

Ms.T: but you didn't know it was me you had feelings for. coulda been anyone

chessman: but it was you, T. who you are doesn't change with a screen name

Ms.T: arrggh. go away, mitchell

chessman: don't bail on me. i NEED to know. find your inner tatiana and talk to me

Ms.T: ok·ok. OK. first of all, i'm a little sorry we tricked you

chessman: ok... thanks, i guess

Ms.T: but if we hadn't, i would never have gotten to know you...

chessman: i know... i hate that :-)

Ms.T: and second. you know what I... love about you most? your feelings really are so deep and so truthful. they really are

chessman: they drive bliss crazy

Ms.T: no, they don't, honey

chessman: and now she's got real reasons to hate me. i'm kinda panicking here

Ms.T: don't even. she's nuts about you

chessman: oh great. oh excellent. and will you put in a good word for me?

Ms.T: lol

EXCHANGE STUDENT ROOM **UNION HIGH SCHOOL**

BoBoy: well, but really. if bridget was there, then bliss was gone. so u didn't c nuthin. hah.

bliss4u: lol. but i was there, meat-head. and ur in big trouble

BoBoy: who was there? which u was there?

bliss4u: i was. ME. the me underneath

alfonso: u dawgs r getting too deep 4 me. i just know it was the best stunt ever pulled

gothling: zackly. excellent scheming

alfonso: excellent puppeteering

gothling: excellent revenge

alfonso: sublime revenge, gurlfriend. gimme 5

gothling: up top

Ms.T: revenge for what, annie?

gothling: i don't know. just revenge on the world

✉ IM from BoBoy

BoBoy: bridget—i mean, bliss?

bliss4u: yikes. what r u doing?

BoBoy: i gotta ask u something

bliss4u: but what if T finds out ur chatting me on the side?

BoBoy: sorry, but i need 2 know. was it the u underneath talking? u know, when u were bridget and i was me?

bliss4u: oh, beau, please

BoBoy: was it? because i thought that was the real thing, i totally thought so. i get these... feelings sometimes

bliss4u: i know u do. ur practically psychic sometimes

BoBoy: so was i right?

bliss4u: oh, it's so confusing. really beau, i can't talk about it

BoBoy: <sigh> k. i know. not yr fault. going away now

bliss4u: no, listen. listen. because there may never be another time to say this

BoBoy: say what?

bliss4u: beau honey, when i was bridget, i did. i really really liked u. it surprised me how much

BoBoy: aw. that helps, bliss. thanks

bliss4u: but i can't keep being bridget, u know

BoBoy: i know. it's ok

bliss4u: thanks. but beau?

BoBoy: yes ma'am?

bliss4u: we can still talk sometimes, can't we?

EXCHANGE STUDENT ROOM **UNION HIGH SCHOOL**

chessman: annie, what revenge on the world?
            what's the world done? what have
            i done to you? ever??

BoBoy: or me. i never did nothing, annie

gothling: look. ur blowing this out of proportion. this
            was all just a bet between me and my gurls

chessman: a bet... about what?

gothling: oh, they were so sick in luv, and i thought
            they needed a reality check

BoBoy: k, i just threw up in my mouth a little

chessman: you hated the idea that they were
            in love??

Ms.T: you're not making this better by dodging
            your guilt, beau

BoBoy: but what am i guilty of?

bliss4u: wait! i know this one! >;)

alfonso: lol, bridget

BoBoy: owww...

chessman: seriously, bliss and T. if you
            set up a false scenario, you can't
            claim what happens there is real

bliss4u: oh, get out. u guys totally cheated on us,
            and that's REAL enuf

BoBoy: man, this is so unfair... u came on 2 us 2
            MAKE us cheat

Ms.T: zackly. and you went for it, romeo. i am SO
            mad at you, even if i did set you up

chessman: know what? i say we take this to bliss's mom. i don't think she'll say it's our fault at all

bliss4u: 4get about it

BoBoy: excellent. T's mom too. she's on my side 4 everything

Ms.T: lol. you're grounded from my mom as of right now. she has no judgment when it comes to you

gothling: anyway, all this proves that i was right. guys r all alike

chessman: oh annie, that is so boring

BoBoy: so contumelious

alfonso: u really believe this, annabelle?

gothling: dude, ur a fine 1 to talk

alfonso: no that's my point. u think they're the same as me?

gothling: sure i do*

Ms.T: ok. hold on. in the 1st place, johnson, let the record show that YOU are not as bad as you pretend. and in the 2nd place, mitch and beau are in deep doo doo because they said THEY were so pure

gothling: zackly. guys r all like this. maybe they mean well, but their minds wander

✉ IM from chessman

chessman: i wasn't THAT easy, was i?

Ms.T: my american darling, i nearly despaired of *ever* winning you ;-)

chessman: lol... no wait. that isn't funny

Ms.T: but i am so mad at beau. did you see how quickly he went for bliss?

✉ IM from BoBoy

BoBoy: so, bliss. how mad do u think T is?

bliss4u: get real. she adores u

BoBoy: well, how do i get her back?

bliss4u: just say u made a mistake. she'll be fine

BoBoy: how about mitch? should i tell him 2 gravel?

bliss4u: lol. yes, tell him 2 gravel

EXCHANGE STUDENT ROOM **UNION HIGH SCHOOL**

alfonso:	ok ok. so annie's inflicted her wisdom. guys r all alike
gothling:	**thank u**
alfonso:	i won't argue with how the creator made us. all guys love all women
BoBoy:	**scuse me, um, <cough> all women, but ESPECIALLY our own woman**
Ms.T:	i wonder what he means by that.... anyone? anyone?
bliss4u:	what happened 2 his nerdy friend, is what i wonder

chessman: \<sigh\> i'm here, ms. bliss

bliss4u: and?

chessman: well, i feel like i just flunked all
            my classes. you guys played a great
            scam on us

bliss4u: funny. i was sure there'd be an apology
            somewhere

chessman: there is, there is...

            ok, bliss, i began to lose hope.
            i thought you had another guy, and
            then i let down my guard. i doubted
            you, and i'm sorry

bliss4u: hmmmph. i don't know...

gothling: **not that i really care, but i should remind certain
            people of the terms of their bet**

bliss4u: get out. i will NOT take him back. not until
            he's been punished

chessman: say what?

gothling: **lol. no, bliss. i don't think that's an option.
            u lost...**

bliss4u: i put this 2 my gurls. should i take him back?
            does he deserve it?

Ms.T: well... he just now groveled. and actually, he
            resisted a loooong time...

chessman: i shouldn't have doubted. won't
            happen again, bliss

Ms T: ...a MUCH longer time than SOME people

BoBoy: **yeah. me too, T. i know i'm a bonehead. lesson
            learned**

Ms.T: boy, i am going 2 pound on you so bad

BoBoy: **yess!**

gothling:	**okokok, let's don't get all weepy**
alfonso:	can i just say 1 thing?
gothling:	**what is it, partner?**
alfonso:	just thinking about trust and faith from the guy's side. when u mess with someone's head like that, u do make it sorta hard 4 them 2 trust u in the future
gothling:	**oh please**
alfonso:	no, really. he'll always ask, is this the girl i love, or is this the one who scammed me?
gothling:	**sweetie. peaches. she's both**
bliss4u:	i don't get it
Ms T:	peaches... <groan>
gothling:	**gurl, if u can only love a perfect guy, ur freakin nuts. and he's crazy too, if he thinks u have only 1 face**
Ms.T:	one mask, you mean?
gothling:	**it's the same thing. we've all got lots. the job of yr sweetheart is 2 luv them all**
BoBoy:	**even the contumelious ones?**
chessman:	well, <ahem> er, bridget, i've always been fascinated with England, what what. do you, um... have any plans for tonight?
bliss4u:	shall we have a spot of tea at my place? we can talk about how grounded ur... maybe play a little chess?
chessman:	i'll just get my board
Ms.T:	look at that. she stole my american husband!
BoBoy:	**tatiana, <ahem> i'm not much of a gypsy, but i, um...**

Ms.T: but you haff a certain feeling for me,
          i thinking

BoBoy: **yes, ma'am, i surely do**

Ms.T: is destiny, my darling. do not fight it

pure poetry

📧 IM from alfonso

JUNE 18 7:30 PM

alfonso: ahem...

gothling: johnson, sup?

alfonso: despinetta, my love

gothling: how's my favorite puppeteer?

alfonso: well. <ahem> annie, i've gotta put this 2 u 1 last time, or i'll never be able 2 face myself in the morning

gothling: why am i suddenly on my guard, i wonder?

alfonso: ur not an easy person 2 get along with, but honestly... well, the truth is i just can't imagine trying with anyone else anymore

gothling: oh, here we go again

alfonso: and don't tell me we're not talking about this

gothling: J, honey, if i needed a guy, u would definitely be on the list. like on page 50

alfonso: annie, get real. u don't need a guy—u need me

gothling: i couldn't trust u, johnson. how obvious is that?

alfonso: i know. i know i deserve that

gothling: so there it is

alfonso: well, no, it doesn't end there. because honestly, gurlfriend, i'm going 2 have trouble trusting u 2

gothling: oh really?

alfonso: are u kidding? we've just been tooling our best friends

gothling: true. and i feel terrible about that... NOT

alfonso: but in case u haven't noticed. about women, i am totally, totally a different person

gothling: r u?

alfonso: u don't know me yet. u can take the chance

gothling: dude, i just don't believe in new leaf stuff. changing stripes and all that

alfonso: eww. listen, if we're going 2 be together, you'll HAVE 2 stop mixing metaphors

gothling: lol. u do amuse me... but no, johnson, we're NOT going 2 be together. i'm telling u, i been there. ate that t-shirt

alfonso: oh, stop. just stop with all this "afraid to love again" stuff

gothling: gimme a break. yr life's a country song. u got a string of broken hearts from here 2 nashville, cowboy

alfonso: and how bout yr life, my frozen queen? u watch other people, but u've forgotten the thrill of yr own feelings

gothling: arrggh. will u stop with this?

alfonso: no, in a word. i won't. listen 2 yr feelings

gothling: look, fool, i don't trust feelings. it's that simple

alfonso: ok, that sounds true, at least

gothling: thank u

alfonso: and what R yr feelings? tell the truth

gothling: oh, u make me so mad

alfonso: that's a start, luv. but why r u mad?

gothling: no. no way will u get me 2 put it in writing

alfonso: aight. we'll go with that 4 now

gothling: fine

alfonso: fine

gothling: fine

alfonso: how about this: i finished yr poem

gothling: my poem? really?

alfonso: yeah, really

gothling: u really wrote me a poem

alfonso: it's like the hardest thing i've ever done. pure poetry

gothling: u really did?

alfonso: and i don't want u making fun of it

gothling: i won't. i won't

alfonso: of course u will. but i don't care

gothling: so where is it? and it's about me?

alfonso: it's sort of about us—not in a sick way

gothling: course not

alfonso: it's a little edgy, a little dark

gothling: show it 2 me. show it 2 me

alfonso: but it's got good structure, a good controlling image. i like it. u probably won't

gothling: are u gonna SHOW it 2 me?

alfonso: oh. right. sorry

ok, close yr eyes

gothling: lol. what's the title?

alfonso: here u go

"A Masked Ball" (for Annie)

Behind the castle, from a deepening sky,
two crows in old tuxedos slide down
the breeze like down a ballroom banister.
They dance alone, to the tune of their own
rough noise. They peck, they scavenge
sticks and strings for toys. Black ribbons.
Worthless shiny things.

Do you think in heaven they have set aside
a room for crows like you and me to whom
the world is only a museum of masks
and rumpled souls ready to be shaken
out and tried? And will we like what we
have seen, when our curiosity is satisfied?

Will we like who we've become behind our
capes and masks and sad lone ranger
eyes?

gothling: johnson, i like this

alfonso: it's a sonnet. did u catch that?

gothling: i like it very much

alfonso: k, i messed up the count in 2 lines, and
the rhymes aren't all where they should be

gothling: it's beautiful. i love it

alfonso: but it's almost a sonnet. it's the best i
can... what? u do?

gothling: i love it

alfonso: oh, gag me, i'm so relieved

gothling: maybe ur not such a chump...

alfonso: awww

gothling: u really r a poet, aren't u?

alfonso: well, when properly inspired...

gothling: awww

alfonso: well

gothling: yeah?

alfonso: well, that's all i wanted

gothling: what is?

alfonso: just 2 give u the poem

gothling: hush, i'm reading it again

alfonso: right. k

gothling: right

alfonso: so that's it then

gothling: shh

alfonso: except. um. so, annie?

gothling: hm?

alfonso: so u got any plans 2nite?

gothling: what?

alfonso: i was just heading 2 the mall

gothling: oh u idiot

alfonso: was that a yes?? it was! it WAS!

gothling: well... buy me a lone ranger mask?

alfonso: we'll buy a pair

gothling: k, pick me up b4 i change my mind

alfonso: YES!

gothling: but johnson

alfonso: annabelle?

gothling: don't think i'll never test u... ;-)

YOUR UNCLE JERRY'S BLOG

Under Construction
19 JUNE

Your Uncle Jerry is currently taking leave of his senses.
    Peace and joy.